Nottinghamshire Children Tell Tales

Volume Four

Published by New Generation Publishing in 2013

Copyright © Nottingham Children 2013

First Edition

 New Generation Publishing

Nottinghamshire Children Tell Tales: Volume Four

Contents

Acknowledgements

No competition would be worth its weight in anything without entries and judges. Over the last four years, we have been privileged in having some fantastically talented and experienced people who have given their time and expertise to judge the stories and poems submitted by Nottinghamshire's young people. They have constantly supported and promoted our efforts in encouraging our young authors and poets to use their imagination and get pen to paper or fingers to keyboard, so my grateful thanks go to Vernon Coaker who is the Member of Parliament for Gedling, Amanda Bowman, Michael Cox, Steve Bowkett, Helen Hollick and Richard Spurr.

In previous books, there has been little information given about our judges and supporters and I would like to rectify that omission now. Over the next few pages you will learn more about these extraordinary people.

Since 2006, we have received cross-party support from a number of Nottinghamshire County Councillors. Without them, New Writers UK could never have grown to the extent it has and it is very doubtful whether this competition would ever have got off the ground. My grateful thanks go to past and present Councillors John Allin, John Clarke, The Hon Joan Taylor, MBE, Alan Rhodes, Jen Cole, Peter Barnes, Michelle Gent, Carol Pepper, Keith Walker, Andy Stewart, David Taylor, Mel Shepherd, Ken Rigby and, if I have forgotten anyone, I am truly sorry for the omission.

Andrew Dobell is the consummate artist who has kindly given his time and talent freely to design each of our cover pictures and we are profoundly grateful to him for his efforts on our behalf.

Daniel Cooke of New Generation Publishing has been involved with each of our books in various ways and has always been a dependable and trusted publisher. I am delighted he has been there for us on each occasion and has also been a great friend and support to New Writers UK since 2006.

Then we have the wonderful members of New Writers UK who have read through the entries each year to carry out short-listing. As, over the years, I have come to know some of our entrants and their families, I no longer take part in short-listing to ensure impartiality. This is not an easy task as no-one wants to disappoint young people but our members carry this procedure out with fairness and objectivity and, as they are authors or copy editors, their opinions are based on experience and expertise. So my thanks go to John Baird, Michael Smedley, Fiona Linday, Lia Ginno, Rachel Littlewood, Awen Little, Gloria Morgan, Alan Dance, Michelle Gent, Pam Littlewood, Steve Taylor and Nick Thom for all their help.

This year we received double the usual number of entries and it is so good to see friends of previous entrants getting involved or word-of-mouth spreading the information around the county about our competition. Childhood imagination is something to be treasured and nurtured as all too soon we grow up and the realities of life take over.

So to the young people of Nottinghamshire I say, keep reading, continue with your writing even if you don't think you have the time. Writing such gloriously imaginative prose and poetry is something to be proud of and talent should always be cherished.

Julie Malone
Editor

Foreword by Vernon Coaker, MP

Co-presenter of the awards to Finalists 2012

Young people's writing can be so inspirational. This collection, I am confident, will inspire those who read it. I am sure also that being part of New Writers UK will spark an interest in writing and will help to maintain that interest into the future, for young and old alike.

I send my heartfelt congratulations to everyone who has taken part in Nottinghamshire and I wish you all well in your future writing.

Biography:

Vernon Coaker is Labour MP for Gedling in Nottinghamshire. He won the seat in 1997, taking it from Conservative Junior Minister Andrew Mitchell with a majority of 3,802. The seat was retained in June 2001 with a majority of 5,598 and then again in 2005 with a majority of 3,811. In the most recent election (May 2010) Vernon Coaker retained the Gedling seat with a majority of 1,859.

In the October 2011 reshuffle, Vernon Coaker was appointed as the Shadow Secretary of State for Northern Ireland. Before this he was appointed Shadow Minister of State for Policing when Labour elected the Shadow Cabinet in September 2010. After the General Election (May 2010) Vernon became the Shadow Minister of State for Schools. Before the 2010 General Election Vernon Coaker was the Minister of State for Schools and learners. He was first appointed to this position in the June 2009 reshuffle. He was previously the Minister of State for Policing, Security and Crime. Before becoming a Minister of State, Vernon was the Under-secretary of State in the Home Office.

Vernon has a Constituency Office in Daybrook, and holds at least four surgeries each month around the constituency and is happy to take up issues on behalf of local people. He also sees constituents at the constituency office, makes a large number of home visits and organises "roving surgeries" and "supermarket surgeries" throughout the constituency.

Before becoming an MP, Vernon Coaker was Deputy Head-teacher at Bigwood School in Nottingham. This was one of four schools at which he taught in the local area. The others were Manvers Pierrepont, Arnold Hill School and Bramcote Park. He had also pursued an active role in local politics as a Borough Councillor.

He is married to Jackie, and they have a daughter and a son. In his spare time his interests include sport – he is a keen Spurs fan – walking in the countryside and current affairs.

Foreword by Michael Cox

Children's author and Co-presenter of the awards to Finalists 2012

Writing is great! It helps you discover all those idea-packed cubby-holes in your brain which you perhaps never even knew you had. It also helps you sort jumbled thoughts into some sort coherent order (not to mention your shopping and 'to-do' lists). And this great 'brain-to-paper' activity enables you to let other people in on all manner of deeply personal thoughts and feelings which you can't convey to them in other ways.

When they produced the wonderful pieces of writing in this anthology I'm sure the young writers had a fantastic time expressing and putting together their ideas. They may even have surprised themselves by producing work they didn't know they were capable of. How wonderful, therefore, it must have been for them to discover their work had been chosen for the anthology.

So well done young writers. And thanks to New Writers UK for making all this great stuff happen. Carry on scribbling ... everyone!

Biography:

Having failed to get past the vicious, armed border guards that patrol the Nottinghamshire countryside, Michael still lives in his home county with his wife, who is a teacher, his cat, which isn't, and various hens and ducks, which couldn't be, even if they wanted to. He's got one son, who is also an author and a journalist.

Michael's spare time activities include walking to his work room, switching on his computer and frightening the postman. When he's not busy writing he's to be found jetting off on exciting, expenses paid research trips to his local library. In addition to this he loves visiting schools and talking to children about writing and fun things to do with dead mammoths. During these visits he also draws pictures, reads from his books and asks school caretakers for directions to the loo.

When he finds the time Michael still likes to go outdoors and paint pictures of trees and sheep but says he gets really irritated when they stroll away before he's finished (that's the sheep, not the trees). He also loves reading and listening to blues and African pop music.

Foreword by Amanda Bowman

Programme Presenter
BBC Radio Nottingham
External Judge 2011 and 2012

It seems a bit impertinent to tell you how much you're going to enjoy what's coming next... you might prefer sloppy grammar, clichés and split infinitives, in which case you've come to the wrong book.

Too many of us think our young people are rude, aggressive, self-centred and lazy. These stories show that a lot of them are totally opposite - the range and skill of these writers will knock your socks off.

There I go again - presuming you're wearing socks! I believe this is the best crop of poetry and stories yet... but it's what you think that counts. I sincerely hope you enjoy this collection as much as I did.

Biography:

Amanda fell into radio in 1986 when she answered an advert for someone who could publicise community groups and ended up on the Careline.

Since then, she has worked for nearly all of the commercial stations in Nottingham and also for a national station where she did the Breakfast show for three years. Not a natural early riser, she found the 0400 wake ups a real challenge.

She has been lucky enough to meet some great and unusual people and her oddest radio moments include waiting for Sir Roger Moore to come out of a gingerbread house, having her shirt photographed by Rod Stewart and singing King of the Swingers to a very startled Kim Wilde.

Alongside radio, Amanda has also worked in a homeless hostel, as a CAB manager, a nanny, a helpline operator, a volunteer coordinator and for a magazine about canals and riverboats - amongst others.

She is married to the long suffering Steve and has two grown up children, Joseph and Susannah.

Her home is a bit of a miniature zoo. One of her proudest achievements is that she has taught her cockatiels to whistle the theme tune to The Flumps.

For the last couple of years Amanda has presented the late show on BBC Radio Nottingham playing music and setting questions and riddles for late night listeners to join in the conversation. So if you're up late at night and wanting good company you couldn't do better than tuning in to Amanda's show. You'll soon see why so many people love her and call in again and again.

(with acknowledgement to BBC Radio Nottingham)

Steve Bowkett.

Author and Hypnotherapist
External Judge 2009, 2010, 2011 and 2012

Biography:

Steve was born and brought up in the mining valleys of South Wales. He started writing for pleasure at the age of thirteen, shortly after moving to the Leicester area, where he still lives.

Steve's background is in education. He taught English for 18 years in Leicestershire High Schools, though is now a full-time writer, storyteller and also a qualified hypnotherapist.

In his time he has written fantasy and SF for teenagers, adult and teen horror, romance, mainstream fiction for pre-teens, fiction and non-fiction for younger readers and poetry for all ages. He has also published a number of educational books, principally in the fields of literacy, creativity, thinking skills and emotional resourcefulness. This year sees the publication of his sixtieth book.

For further information on Steve, please visit
www.stevebowkett.co.uk

Helen Hollick

Highly acclaimed Historical author
External Judge 2009, 2010, 2011 and 2012

Biography:

Helen lives on the outskirts of NE London, England, close to Epping Forest with her husband and adult daughter – and a variety of pets, although she is hoping to move to Devon in the New Year – as it is her 60th Birthday in 2013 a new home, new life will be a lovely birthday present!

Helen has been passionate about books and writing all her life. Her first employment was in a local library, where she discovered the history behind the legends of King Arthur, which eventually led to the writing of her *Pendragon's Banner Trilogy*, the first of her historical novels.

Helen has been Chair of the local Dyslexia Association and worked part-time as a School Librarian in a Special Needs school. She especially enjoyed encouraging new writers to achieve their dream of writing a novel. Her best advice? *'To finish, you must first get started!'*

Helen was first published by William Heinemann (Random House UK) but when her books were not to be re-printed she obtained the copyright and re-published with a small UK independent company as part of their even smaller mainstream imprint. The company recently closed, however, so rather than fall out of print again here in the UK, Helen republished with an assisted publishing company, SilverWood Books, based in Bristol.

Helen's Historical Fiction novels are also published in the US by Sourcebooks Inc. and she was delighted to make the USA Today best seller list with *The Forever Queen*.

For Helen, writing began with reading – one of her earliest memories is coming out of the library clutching a book: she was about four. When Helen was thirteen she desperately wanted a pony. As she could not afford one, she made one up, fulfilling her dream through writing stories. Helen had her pony – she was called Tara and they had many exciting adventures together (She confesses she often used to write my stories when she should have been paying attention to class lessons!) It did not occur to her at the time that making up stories was not a common thing to do. Didn't everyone enter the world of imagination via the scribbled pages of various stories? Helen was quite shocked when she discovered that no, they didn't.

Helen still inhabits the Realm of the Imaginary when she writes her novels today. Helen's characters, to her, are real people, their adventures are real adventures. And Helen is delighted to be able to encourage other youngsters to follow their own paths into that wonderful place called Imagination – what a dull place the real world be without Imagination!

Main website www.helenhollick.net
Facebook: www.facebook.com/helen.hollick
Twitter: http://twitter.com/HelenHollick

Author of:
The Pendragon's Banner Trilogy (the 'what might have really happened' story of King Arthur)

A Hollow Crown (UK title) / The Forever Queen (US title)
Harold the King (UK title) / I am the Chosen King (US title)
(The first two books of a proposed trilogy regarding the people and events that led to 1066 and the Battle of Hastings – probably the most famous date in English history)

The Sea Witch Voyages:
Voyage One: Sea Witch
Voyage Two: Pirate Code
Voyage Three: Bring it Close
Pirate-based adventures with a touch of fantasy or Hornblower meets Richard Sharpe and Indiana Jones – at sea. If you enjoyed the Pirates of the Caribbean movies, you will love these.

Richard Spurr
Radio Presenter
External Judge 2012

Biography:

Born and bred in Nottingham, Richard was educated at Nottingham High School and then spent three years amongst the fens of East Anglia studying modern languages and literary theory - the obvious choice for a broadcaster.

After several years in London working in TV production and as a voiceover artist, he decided he could resist the urge of the airwaves no longer and headed back up the M1. Richard joined BBC Radio Nottingham as a Travel News Reporter in 2005.

He has always been transfixed by the wireless, and has an unhealthily extensive knowledge of old British comedy, with a particular penchant for the likes of 1960s radio comedy Round The Horne and Ealing-made film School For Scoundrels.

Outside the world of broadcasting, Richard's consuming passions are food and wine. He invested in a Chinese cookery book, a wok, and a cleaver, at the age of eight and never looked back. Seafood is one of his greatest loves and obsessions.

(with acknowledgment to BBC Radio Nottingham)

Group One

Primary School Years

Four to Six

A NORMAL DAY GOES WRONG

A COMPLETELY NORMAL DAY

I awoke one morning, expecting today to be like any other. I got dressed, had breakfast and brushed my teeth. Now I just needed a normal day at school. But, before I left for school, my younger brother picked up a garden gnome and threw it. It just so happened that three LEGO men were lying on the grass, next to the gnome. The gnome bounced off the trampoline and scattered some peculiar powder on the ground, and some fell on the LEGO men. I was sitting in the car by this time, and therefore didn't notice three small – well, tiny actually – men climbing into my school bag. And, for that reason, I got a big shock when they climbed out of my school bag during a SATS paper! And they were ALIVE – definitely not normal. My normal day had got off to a very bad start.

BREAKTIME?

Being lonely in the playground is no longer a problem, as Bill, Frank and Joe (that's what the LEGO men called themselves), demonstrated during morning break. Unfortunately, they'd packed a toy car in my school bag which meant spending play time repeatedly catching the car. Luckily for me, they were driving a Ford Fiesta, which isn't very quick. But as a precaution, I reckon I'd better hide my toy Ferrari Enzo.

OOPSIES!

The rest of my day was continually disrupted by Bill, Frank and Joe. At lunchtime I found out they'd scoffed all my lunch. After school, I confiscated the gnome (and, of course the Ferrari Enzo). Oopsies! I spilt some powder on a LEGO Hero Factory set. In case you don't already know, LEGO Hero Factory sets are very fun to play with and come in two types; heroes and villains. Unfortunately, the powder spilt on the villains. Typical! Perhaps, if I hadn't thrown away the instruction booklet, I may have known their names.

DARKNESS AND DOOM

The black one was by far the biggest. It held a staff in its hand and used it to suck the light from my room. His evil blue eyes glowed. Then I saw it on the top shelf - the powder. I had a plan. The evil black villain stamped his foot, and his two evil accomplices crawled out from under my bed. Their heads were like orange and blues skulls glowing in the light from the staff. I desperately searched around looking for an escape but the door was padlocked, the window was barred and, to make it worse, Bill, Frank and Joe were locked in a cage. Then a sudden thought struck me. Heroes defeat villains.

HEROES EMERGE VICTORIOUS   (HOPEFULLY)

But my plan had a loophole. To get the heroes, I needed powder. And to get to the powder, I needed heroes and, to get heroes, (See what I mean?) I needed powder. Well, for once, my little brother's cowboy costume came in useful. Well, the hat was too small, and the pistol was broken (It wasn't real anyway) but all I needed was the lasso. But finding a lasso is difficult with three powerful robots staring at you, and three guns pointing at you, (even though they were quite small).

A COWBOY, A GNOME, AND A LEGO FIGURE

Well you've probably guessed it by now that this isn't a 'completely normal day' as planned. In fact, it was getting less normal by the second. Of course, for this story to have a happy ending, I would have to lasso the gnome. And, luckily for fans of 'happily ever after', I did. But, luckily for fans of tense climaxes, the gnome slipped through my grip and straight into the waiting arms of the big, black villain.

BUTTERFINGERS!

The 'butterfingers' in this chapter isn't me. It's the big, black villain. The gnome slipped through his grip too, and would've smashed if it hadn't landed on the head of a hero. Now it was up to him (or her, I don't really know). Hero versus villain!

HERO VERSUS VILLAIN: THREE SETS OF 'CUFFS

It was only when I removed the gnome from the head of the hero (he/she was green, by the way) I realised Bill, Frank and Joe were no longer in the cage. And the villains were no longer on the carpet. But with implemented radar and a camera mounted helmet, the green hero found my LEGO men in precisely 5.765014329 seconds. Each had a pair of 'cuffs and each was staring into the face of a villain.

THE BATTLE FOR A HAPPY ENDING

With super speed and fantastic flexibility, Breez (as she called herself) soon had the blue villain caught and 'cuffed. But by this time, the orange one had attached a jetpack to himself and had soared up into the air. But brave Breez was one step ahead, and jumped off the top shelf. She landed on the orange villain and had 'cuffed him, quick as a flash. But the black villain's staff sucked Breez way from the two 'cuffed villains, and towards his clutches. Victory was his for the taking.

PERIL AND PRESTON

Breez shut her eyes, and expected the worst but the worst never came. A white hero accompanied by four others said, in a questioning voice (and a strong American accent), "Do you want to put your hands up, Von Nebula? I am Preston Stormer, these are the other Hero Factory heroes and you're caught and 'cuffed." And a few seconds later, Von Nebula was.

EPILOGUE

And they all lived happily ever after...well? What did you expect?

By Ben Holdstock

DIAMOND JUBILEE DISASTER

My name is Clover–Rose Mason and I am the Head Housekeeper for Her Majesty, Elizabeth II Queen of England. Her Diamond Jubilee is less than two weeks away and everyone in the palace is a bit frantic, as you would expect.

Anyway back to me, my job is to make sure everyone in the palace does what they're supposed to do. If people are ill, I take over their job as well. Last week I was supposed to cook a banquet for all the Queen's closest friends and family but, and please don't tell anyone, I can't cook so I got a professional in to do it for me. Now there's just one week to go until the Jubilee, the banquet went perfectly, everyone enjoyed themselves and more parties have been happening all over the country. Everyone is in the mood for a good time.

One morning I woke up and went to check on Her Majesty, but when I went in she had a raspy cough, an incredibly high fever and a bucket beside her bed full of smelly, disgusting vomit. I called the palace doctor immediately and told him to come quickly. When he arrived he checked her temperature, emptied the bucket of vomit and opened the tinted window. He looked back at me and said,

"She's awfully sick. She needs at least two weeks rest. It's because of the exhaustion of the Jubilee. You have got to remember, she's 86 years old."

I suddenly realised that she would not be able go to the Diamond Jubilee celebration but someone needed to be on the balcony to wave to everyone. And it had to be the Queen.

I started to think about we could do. The only idea that popped into my head was to get a lookalike to pretend to be the Queen for the day. I searched the Internet for someone who looked most like the Queen and was just about to give up when my cat, Lady, jumped on my computer mouse and it scrolled down. I picked her up and put her on the floor but when I looked up, there on the screen was a lady who looked exactly the same as the Queen, apart from a crooked nose, and that could be looked past, so I telephoned her and asked her to be at Buckingham Palace at 9:30am the next day wearing a hat or scarf to keep her face hidden. She could not be noticed.

In the morning I found the lady waiting outside the palace and showed her what to do, how to do it and told her when to be there. Then we just had to wait for the week to end.

On the day of the Jubilee we got into our places and the crowds arrived. Everyone in London was there but one little girl stuck out from the crowd. She had long black hair and skin as dark as a raven's feather, her dark brown eyes showed me her whole personality and, when she stretched out her arms to feel the wind, it looked as though she was just about to fly off into the sunset. She only looked about four years old but was very curious about the Queen.

After she had stared at her for a while, she shouted at the top of her voice,

"That's not the Queen!" Everyone fell silent and stared at the lookalike and realised the little girl was right. I was sacked from my old job at the palace but as I had tried so hard to help Her Majesty and save the Diamond Jubilee, I was given a new job as Royal Adviser to the Queen.

P.S. I'm now a happy member of the Royal Family. I married Prince Harry. If you were wondering what happened to the little girl, it turned out she was an orphan named Raven who had been taken there by her foster parents. Harry and I adopted her and now we are a happy Royal Family. And our Raven will never leave us just as the ravens will never leave the Tower of London.

By Erin Hayball

THE PHOTO

The clock was ticking – I knew I needed to find my identity card to get to work. I couldn't get into the building without it. The anger was starting to rise inside me. Where was a possible place to put it? I yanked open my junk draw. But, something caught my eye, it was a faded and creased – it was a photograph. It brought back memories – powerful memories.

There I was, on the day of the wedding in 1998,

"Mum I know the truth behind Colin. He's evil," I shouted at her. Mum stepped into her wedding dress and took a deep breath and said, "Rose this is just one of your silly stories."

She reached for her lip gloss and said, "I know he will be the perfect Step-dad for you." My bridesmaid dress felt awfully tight. I walked out of the dressing room to find myself standing next to Colin.

"What are you doing here?" I asked him.

"I'm waiting for your Mum," he replied. I raised my eyebrows. There was an odd twinkle in his eye – it was obvious he was up to something. He walked away. I thought something was going to happen – there was that feeling in the air.

Mum and I were feeling very nervous. I picked up Mum's train and she walked gracefully down the aisle with me behind. But, when I looked at Colin, there was an odd gleam in the back pocket of his trousers. What was it?

"Mum Colin's got something in his pocket," I yelled. My Auntie Glenda grabbed my arm and whispered in my ear, "Calm down Rose, Colin's not any trouble." She pushed me back into place but I wasn't convinced. I sat picking my nails while they said their vows. Then something happened that none of us expected. They were about to kiss. Mum had tears of happiness running down her face, while Colin looked just about normal – there wasn't even a smile of happiness on his face. My Mum reached forward. Colin swiftly pulled something silver and gleaming from his back pocket. Mum screamed as she backed away.

He moved quickly towards Mum, while saying, "Did you really think I would want to marry you, Susan Murphy? You really thought that didn't you?" By now my Mum had bright red cheeks and tears were rolling down onto her dress. All the guests were cowering away from Mum and Colin – I was one of them. Colin walked towards Mum, she moved back towards the window but she couldn't move back anymore as Colin was cowering over her, moving closer, inch by inch...

"Mum I love you!" I shouted.

"I love you too," Mum whispered.

Ah-ah, there was my identity card. Who would have thought of putting on the key-hook? I placed Mums photo on top of the bureau – after all, I needed to take care of it. The photo was one of the few things I had left of my mother. I looked at the clock. It read 8:30am on the 28 July 2012; I was late and I needed to get to work.

By Malaika Mathieson

HIDDEN

"You must hide it well...don't even let them know as they will learn when the time is right." There was a crash – the door at the bottom of the tower had fallen inwards.

"Go now!"

"No! Come with us," she begged.

"I am as good as dead. They know I am here..."

Footsteps could be heard coming up the stairs.

"Get them out of here now!" he whispered whilst pressing something into her hand.

With tears in her eyes, she opened the trapdoor and led two children down the narrow steps. They reached the bottom of the tower and scurried cautiously into the woods. Screams could be heard from the tower.

"Find them! I want it! Don't let them live!"

But they kept going, deeper and deeper into the forest. Not once did they look back, knowing that now, nothing would ever be the same.

10 Years later

Lidia strolled into their apartment and saw her mum lying on the bed. She offered her some bread.

"Thank you dear," Lidia's mum cleared her throat as she thought about the right words for this difficult situation.

"Well um...I....you know I love you dear and well....Oh...I knew this day would come. I really need to tell you the truth!" by this time Lidia's body was shaking.

"The truth about what, mum?"

"First of all your mum is still alive. She didn't die in the tower like your father and...and...you have a brother."

After an hour Lidia slowly began to unravel what she had heard.

"My real mum is in hiding and I have a brother... but he's on the other side of the country. My father was rich and supposedly had a magic stone that he gave to his wife when his brother

Rovicer tried to steal it. My mother took me and my brother, hid the stone, and separated us forever."

"Well no, not forever dear. You are going to see him tomorrow."

"Why have you been hiding this from me mum? Oh....I guess I'd better call you Portia now because you aren't my real mum, are you?"

"Your mother told me not to tell you until the time was right to do so." Portia stopped for a moment to compose herself and began to explain that Lidia's uncle, Rovicer, was trying to trace the stone again after finding a vital clue and that she had arranged for Lidia to meet her brother tomorrow.

The Next Day
The noise of the train was tremendously loud as it came to a halt and Lidia stepped onto the platform. A tall, smartly dressed man approached her.

There was so much to say but for the first time in her life, Lidia was speechless. As they were driven to the mansion, Arion, Lidia's brother, told her everything that had happened over the past few days.

"I found a clue four days ago and realised that the stone's power is to give you to what you need the most."

"Why does our uncle want it then?" asked Lidia.

"Wouldn't you want a stone that gave you what you wanted?"

"If we find the stone, we could use it to find our mother, that's what we really need, isn't it?" asked Lidia as she puzzled over her brother's response.

"Umm, yes of course," he replied.

In the course of the next few weeks, Lidia and Arion had no luck in finding any more clues as to where the stone might be.

"Our mother might have given you a clue when she left you," coaxed Arion.

"Wouldn't she have given you a clue as well then?" Lidia felt under pressure.

"I don't have a clue!" and he stormed out of the room.

11

Lidia did have something from her real mother but since Arion had been acting weirdly, she decided not to tell him.

Sneaking around
A few hours later Arion left the mansion and Lidia went up to his room. As she sneaked around, she noticed some letters lying on the table so she picked them up and started to read.

This is taking too long. You said you could get information out of anyone and I want the stone now! If you want the money – get me the information. Time is running out for YOU Rovicer.

It was signed *'Portia'*.

That was it. Lidia now knew she couldn't trust anyone. She was on her own. Escaping the mansion was easy, there were so many exits. Of course she took all the supplies she would need and all the money she could find, which was a considerable amount but she had no idea of where she was going.

Lidia had thought that maybe her handkerchief, which was the only thing her real mother had given her, could be a clue. There was an embroidered picture of a cave at the bottom right hand corner, and around the cave were the words,

Woods are green, sea is blue,
But in the middle you find what is true,
It points to what you need for you,
It's in the cave on the Isle of Blue.

The Isle of Blue
The Isle of Blue was a small, sleepy island but still big enough to get lost in. Lidia went around asking if anyone had seen the picture on her handkerchief before. Just as she was about to give up, an old man appeared to recognise it.

"You all been looking for that?" the man grumbled.

"What do you mean?"

"The same two head up to that cave every mornin' an' night for as long as I can remember. Seems like they're waitin' for something."

Lidia ran, hoping that she would find the truth. As she entered the cave a light shone from the middle of the darkened hollow. It shone upon a shimmering pool which reflected the two faces she *needed* to find. Her mother and brother! Lost deep beneath the water was the stone, looking like any other and lost forever. For the first time since the tower she was truly happy.

As for Portia and Rovicer......Well, that's another story!

by Trinity Daniels

WALTER, THE MIND-READING TORTOISE

In a tall house down Frenton Street, a ten year old boy named Henry was reading an interesting book called, 'How to Train Your Tortoise' when there was a knock at the door.

In his house a simple knock meant a big commotion. First, it meant that Henry's tortoise called Walter would wake up startled. Then Henry would run to the door and probably step on Walter at the same time. Walter would then yelp and finally Henry would open the door.

"Good morning!" said the postman brightly, "here are your letters."

One thing I must mention is that Henry's father is rich. He's got paintings, he's got jewellery and lots of silver but this isn't a big part of Henry's life, no, that's Walter's role.

A second important thing, not to be shared, that only Henry knows is that Walter can read minds!

Henry discovered this one day two years ago when he was doing his maths homework. He was stuck on a tricky question and Walter, as he could read minds, could tell Henry was frustrated and motioned for Henry to go with him to the window. Over the road the cleverest kid in his school was also doing his homework. Walter read his mind and demonstrated the answer and since then it has been their little secret. But, that's definitely enough of that and so on with the story.

Henry thanked the postman and took his post and was about to close the door when Walter twitched. That meant something was up with the postman. Walter needed to read his mind for a bit longer so Henry decided to make something up quickly.

"Nice weather isn't it! Makes a change?" Henry exclaimed. The postman looked at the sky and mumbled, "Um, yes it does," he straightened up and said, "Well, nice to see you but I must be getting on my way, there's lots to do!" He picked up his bike and rode into the distance leaving Henry and Walter at the door.

"I only hope that that was long enough for Walter," Henry thought. He closed the door and noticed out of the corner of his eye Walter nodding his scaly head. Henry laughed and carried on reading.

The rest of the day went quickly. Henry and Walter played a few games and watched a bit of TV and soon it was time for tea. Henry wandered into the kitchen and sniffed as he opened the door. Ooh! Pancakes! Henry's favourite. He gobbled one up along with another couple too, then stretched his arms, picked up Walter and put him on the table. It was time for Walter's tea. Henry poured some water and got some food. He looked at the clock, time for bed; he'd leave Walter to finish. Henry slowly went upstairs to his room and relaxed for the night.

"I must stay up, I must," thought Walter as he finished his water. Walter had read the postman's mind and knew he was coming to steal all the jewellery in just thirty minutes time. Walter thought and thought. What to do? But just as a window shattered and the postman came tumbling down Walter had made up his mind...the one that no human could read. Quickly, he lay still, as if asleep as the postman crept slowly into the kitchen towards him.

"This is where it's hidden," he thought and obviously Walter did too. Suddenly Walter made his move. As if poked in the back he pushed all the leftover flour from the pancakes all over the crouching postman. The Postman jumped up and yelled out angrily. Soon Henry and his family were down.

"My golly!" cried Henry's father. They saw the man and rang the police straight away.

"Well done Walter!" said Henry's mother excitedly, "How on earth did you do that?" Well, only Henry and you could possibly know that!!

By Matthew Drury

15

UNBELIEVABLE TEKKERS

Tom grabbed his last birthday present. It was wrapped in a peculiar paper which was virtually torn to shreds. Inquisitively, he looked all over the unusual package but there was no label or sign. Who could it possibly be from? Anyway, Tom didn't care who it was from so he ripped open the box. Inside the box was a football, just an ordinary football! Tom glanced over at his mum, slightly disappointed. As he turned back around to pick up the ball he spotted a note attached to it. The note said,

I am no ordinary ball in many different ways. Furthermore I will respond magically to your touch only. I am a unique football that will never fail at the times you need most to succeed.

Racing quickly, Tom carried the ball out into the garden but could not figure out why it was so special. He was out there all day until he finally remembered what the message had said. *"At the times you need most to succeed."* Tom whispered to himself as his mum came charging outside shouting him in for his dinner.

After dinner Tom hurried straight to bed but he couldn't stop worrying about the important football match he was playing in the following morning. Impressively, Tom's team were top of the league but only by one point and in the morning they were playing the team currently in second place. If only he could use his new football in that crucial game.

Eventually when morning came, Tom was quick to wake up. He got all his kit on ready and dashed into the garden. If only he could work out what magic powers the ball had!

A couple of hours later it was almost time for kick-off. Nervously both teams walked out onto the pitch. You could cut the atmosphere with a knife!

The game began with both teams desperate to win but with the biggest stroke of luck one of the players kicked the ball over the fence and there was no replacement other than Tom's magic ball. Tom ran over to the referee and told him he had a spare football in the car so Tom's dad rushed over to the car and brought back Tom's ball. Tom was delighted! With the game back underway astonishingly as soon as Tom made his first clearance him and his team found themselves 1-0 up as the magic ball drifted left and right in the air and left the keeper watching in disbelief. By half-time, incredibly, Tom's team were 4-0 up and Tom had already scored 3 extraordinary goals. The second half was just as thrilling with endless goals being hammered into the back of the opposition's net. Tom had more than doubled his score as he had now scored 8 sensational goals. The full time whistle blew and the opposition team were left dumbfounded! Tom was a hero (or so everyone thought).

Over the next few weeks, Tom's magical ball was used regularly in all his matches and Tom continued to score an unimaginable amount of goals. However, his immediate improvement on the pitch was beginning to raise suspicion amongst the other players on his own team. In particular his good friend Joe, who used to be the player who scored most of the goals was becoming increasingly jealous of Tom's continuous success and he had a hunch it had something to do with Tom's new ball.

The following Saturday, Tom's team were preparing for a cup final game and the players were getting ready in the changing rooms. Creeping into the changing room sneakily, Joe headed towards Tom's kit bag where Tom kept his precious magic ball. Making sure no one was watching he swapped Tom's ball for another identical one.

A short while later the cup final game began. To start off Tom's team looked a little shaky however that was soon forgotten when Tom dribbled the ball past all the defenders and pulled the trigger and fired a phenomenal shot right in the top corner of the net. You could have heard a pin drop. The crowd were blown away! Never had they seen anything like it before. After the shocked silence, an almighty roar was unleashed by the spectators. Then the referee blew the final whistle.

Joe stood rooted to the spot and could not believe he had doubted his friend's ability. He felt ashamed and embarrassed about how he had treated his team mate.

Back in the changing rooms Tom noticed Joe was unusually quiet. Concerned about his friend, Tom wandered over to Joe and asked him if he was ok. Joe told Tom how he had swapped his special ball and how jealous he had been of his friends amazing performances on the pitch. Tom was very understanding of his friend's behaviour and even shared his secret of the magic ball with him.

Tom had discovered that he didn't need the magic football to be at the top of his game. However the ball had given him the confidence and self-belief to become an exceptional player with an exciting future ahead.

By Jamie Freestone

THE TIME-O-TRON 2000

I pressed the glittering green button and the door of the Time-O-Tron 2000 opened. I stepped inside the gorgeous gold room. Today I wanted to go to the Great Exhibition so I pressed the date pads to 1851AD and spun the location wheel to the Crystal Palace. Then I pressed the Go button.

But...The Time-O-Tron 2000 malfunctioned! The siren wailed and the time machine spun me furiously around like a rag doll. I felt like I was on a carousel going round at 1,000,000 miles an hour. I felt as though I was going to be SICK!!! Then the time machine landed with a loud THUD. Where was I? I pressed the open button cautiously wondering what was in the wilderness.

When I peeped out I was surrounded by towering tall trees, lush green shrubbery and beautiful colourful flowers. Then I stepped out into the shimmering sun light and onto lush, gorgeous green grass and saw a big bright beautiful palace in front of me.

Then to my horror I saw two mean looking guards marching towards me. They were dressed in Tudor clothes. I was NOT! They arrested me for wearing purple, wearing trousers and trespassing and threw me into the Tower of London. They locked the door with a clunk. I was TRAPPED! Help! Then...

I heard a loud cough from the pitch black corner of the room. I nervously investigated. It was a miserable man. I said,

"Hello, I am Hannah. What is your name?"

He replied,

"I am Sir Walter Raleigh and I have been put in here because I married without Queen Elizabeth's permission. What on earth are you wearing?"

I explained, "Trousers and purple...because I am from the year 2012."

Then I see a big bag with leaves sticking out. I asked, "What is in the bag?"

"Potatoes," he replied.

"Why are the leaves on?"

"Because you eat them," he said.

"You do *not* eat them! They are poisonous! You eat the bottom of it."

Then Sir Walter Raleigh understood.

"That was why everyone was ill after the royal banquet! But Potatoes have been banned from court now."

"In 2012 kids love them...but as CHIPS!" I told him. Then I had an idea.

A little later the guards came and took me to the Queen. She didn't look like her pictures. She was covered in Smallpox scars and had poisonous white lead make up and she wore a big orange wig. I was very nervous. What was going to happen?

The Queen asked lots of questions about me and how I got there and she obviously didn't believe me when I said I was from 2012 as she said,

"To prove it, you will cook me something from the future. BUT if I do not like it, you will go back to the Tower of London while I think of a punishment."

I went back to the Tower to get the potatoes then the guards took me to the massive Tudor kitchen. It was bigger than my house! There were lots of people in there and a lady wearing a white apron came up to me and said,

"Good Morrow, I am Mistress McDonald and I will help you."

I explained I was going to cook burger and chips. She looked confused and very worried when she saw the potato leaves. I got busy cooking. I made two circles of bread then I cooked the meat and cut a round piece then put it in the bread. A BURGER!

Next I peeled the potatoes, cut them long and thin then put them in a pan with goose fat and cooked them. CHIPS! After that I shook some salt on them and I was ready to serve burger and chips to the Queen.

Everyone fell silent while Queen Elizabeth tasted the food. Then...she smiled. I could see her blackened and yellowed teeth. She said,

"I love them!!! You are free to go, as long as you give Mistress MacDonald the recipe and here is a penny for your work."

I felt relieved to go home but sad to leave, because I had made friends like Sir Walter Raleigh. I walked quickly across the lush, gorgeous green grass and back to the Time-O-Tron 2000.

When I got inside I put the penny in my drawer then set the date pads to 2012 and spun the location wheel to 'Home'. BUT... the time machine malfunctioned (again!).

Where will I end up this time? Will I have to save my life again?!

Epilogue

My story is made up but parts of it are true.

1585 – Queen Elizabeth I knighted Walter Raleigh.

1589 – Legend has it that Sir Walter Raleigh gave the potato plant to Queen Elizabeth as a gift. There was a royal banquet with potatoes, but the cooks served boiled stems and leaves (which are poisonous) and made everyone ill. Potatoes were banned from court.

1592 – Queen Elizabeth I sent Sir Walter Raleigh to the Tower of London for getting married without her permission.

1851 – The Great Exhibition opened at the Crystal Palace.

By Hannah Greensmith

FOOTBALL!!!

Remain focused when the other team scores
Manage your impulsivity not to break the law
You need to trust your team and believe
Because you don't know what you're doing to achieve
Be patient and your time will come
The passion for your team beats like a drum
You may think you're going down
But you might be parading back into town

Dream hard – and make that dream reality
Think hard – and make thoughts a speciality
We have come so far and we can't afford a disaster
Now we are here we can become the master
If we can bear to hear the future that's been wrote
We will know if our team sails like a boat
To be the best and beat the rest

I believe in my team!!!

By Tom Kirk

ALONE IN PARIS

IN THE BEGINNING

This huge tragedy, all began when young Marco was born. He lived with his Mother and his Father in a posh flat in Paris. Marco lived happily there until the age of nine. Unfortunately, not long after his ninth birthday, his parents experienced a terrible car crash and suffered a number of days and nights in hospital. After two weeks Marco's parents finally passed away. And Marco was left alone, alone in Paris.

Early in the morning, Marco awoke to the sound of the nanny hearing about the terrible news from the postman. Soon after that, Marco heard the nanny leave with all her possessions and wondered what he should do. At first he wondered where his parents had gone but then he thought about going outside. He had never been outside before; his mother always said it was a dangerous place for a young boy but today his parents were not around (and wouldn't be coming back). Marco decided to eventually leave the comfort of his home for the scary outside world. I wonder what he might find?

As Marco opened the door for the first time he was struck with a fresh smell of a bakery and hit with the sound of a herd of bustling people. With fright he slammed the door shut and stopped to take a breath. After a couple of minutes he opened the door again and this sight he never forgot.

A BUSY PARIS DAY

Now Marco was hungry. He looked out to see women jumping in and out of taxis, he'd never seen so many people. The sun shimmered onto his skin as he took a big breath of air and set out to find some breakfast.

Later on he heard the clock strike 9.00 and all the shop signs changed from closed to open. He was delighted and decided to go in local bakery and get some bread. He walked in to the shop and said:

"Here Mister, please can I have some bread?" asked Marco, eyeing the baguettes.

"Of course, anything for a young paying lad," the man behind the counter answered. Marco's heart sunk. Money! No-one ever told him he needed money for food.

"I haven't got any money, sir," replied Marco, wiping away tears.

"No money, then no bread. I don't want some poor tramp in my shop. Get out you, GET OUT!"

Marco was starving now and it was getting dark so he started to walk home. Home? Which way was home? Was it...left? No...right? Forward...maybe? It was hopeless Marco was lost. Luckily Marco found a doorstep on a house where the roof stuck out too far so at least he knew he could stay dry during the night. He was now scared, terrified in fact, and there was nothing he could do but go to sleep and hope for a better day tomorrow.

FOUND A FRIEND

Marco awoke to find an old dog licking his face! What a way to start the morning! But he thought it was funny and bust out laughing. "Hee hee, silly dog. Hee ha he ha," chuckled Marco but he realized he had never been so hungry.

"Hey boy do you think you could find us some food? Can you?" asked Marco grinning.

As quick as a flash the dog disappeared but soon came back with a mighty pile of <u>raw </u>chicken...

And, as you could have guessed Marco scoffed the chicken whole! But I can assure you that did him more harm than good.

FINAL DAYS

It was his tenth birthday that day but Marco was too ill to care. His head ached; he felt sick and had the most horrendous tummy ache. Marco knew it, he thought living by himself would have been a struggle but he never guessed it would this bad. His final day had arrived.

The dog was crying like a baby and all Marco could think about was why did Mam leave me? Until he cried himself to sleep... but the problem was Marco never woke up.

By Yasmin Kowal

Group Two

Secondary School

Years Seven and Eight

THE SACRED LAND

Though shaken beyond anything, I wasn't fully unprepared when the gunshots were heard out my bedroom window for the first time. Bombs were raining down on The Sacred Land after just ten minutes, turning the city I knew so well into a fiery hell. Food and water. A gun! They were my priorities.

"Enyo? Enyo!"

I ignored my mum as I shoved some necessities into a bag. I added a first aid kit, for good measure, and some matches. I doubted I was ever going to come back to this house again.

"Enyo! Where are you? Can you hear me?"

I couldn't keep my mum waiting any more. I knew she wouldn't leave without me, and pretty soon my house would be up in flames too. I grabbed my trainers and a hoodie, and ran down the stairs, my rucksack banging against my leg.

"Mum?"

"Here." My mother was on the verge of tears, but wouldn't let them show. Not yet, anyway. "Take your brother."

I nodded, firmly, taking Levi's small tan hand in my own pale one.

"You know the shelter."

I nodded yet again. Wars were common in The Sacred land, so there were shelters scattered round the city. We had moved from house to house God knows how many times because of it. I guess it was just another thing I had to deal with.

"Go! Now! Before this war gets any worse."

"Mum?"

"Go! I'll meet you at the shelter!"

I bit my lip, wanting to say something meaningful. If my mother got killed in the war, I wanted to have said something. But there was no time. If I didn't leave soon, we would all be ashes.

"Okay. I'll see you there."

I turned towards Levi. "Ready?"

"Where are we going...?" He yawned, rubbing his eyes. He was in bed and sound asleep when the first bomb dropped. Could he not sense that there was something wrong in the air, the feeling of tension that something awful was going to happen? No, I answered myself, He couldn't. He's too innocent, blissfully ignorant.

"Just to the shelter, there's another fight. It's nothing to worry about."

A quick nod of the head told me he understood, then sleep won over as his eyelids drooped shut and his head flopped over onto my hip. I hoisted him up onto my back, ripping off a long thin strip of cloth from my hoodie and using it to tie his limp body to mine. I need my hands free to run properly.

"Enyo! Take Levi, leave while you can!"

I ran to door, turning before I could open it. "I'll see you at the shelter, won't I?"

"Yes, both me and your father. Go! Now!"

I spun on my heel and swung open the front door. I had seen The Sacred Land in war before. I was preparing myself for the worst. But nothing could have ever prepared me for this.

The flames were licking up every building around us, filling the air with toxic smoke. The sun that normally bathed us in warm, pale light was glowing red, and unnaturally swollen with the fumes, choking the city in a fiery hot blaze.

People! I saw them in the distance, armed with guns, firing at each other. I wasn't sure if they could even see what they were doing, I wasn't certain if they were friend or foe. Frankly, I didn't care.

I need to get to the shelter. That was my priority. Keep Levi safe! Keep him alive, even if no one else lived. He wouldn't die! I made myself that promise there and then. He would survive this war, even if it meant killing myself and countless others in the process, selfish as that may seem. With that promise fresh in my mind, I took a deep breath and bolted through the flames.

I could feel my rucksack against my leg, bashing it, gun in my hand. Levi was waking up, but how could anyone sleep through this? He was shouting something but I couldn't hear him, and I know he shouldn't breathe in the smoke.

"Just stay quiet!" I scream. Big mistake! Just that short sentence made me gasp at the air for breath as I was running so quickly, and I breathed in much more of the smoky fumes than was healthy, making me cough and splutter.

"Enyo!"

I heard that, I heard Levi shout my name, but I was coughing so much, and the smoke was making my eyes sting, blurring my vision, and I didn't realise it, but I was hungry, and tired, and oh, I just wanted to sleep...

I realised I wasn't going to be able to go on like this. Levi was shouting frantically, and footsteps that I had only just noticed were drawing closer and closer. I used my last ounce of strength to pull myself behind one of the very few buildings that was not yet alight, and allowed myself a minute or two of rest.

"Enyo? Are you okay?" My nine year old brother's face was filled with concern, and terror. Pure terror!

"I'm fine, really," I reassured him. "I just breathed in too much of the smoke. I'll have a sip of water and rest for a minute..." I slumped to the ground, sipping the water in quietly, enjoying my brief moment of peace. Levi broke the silence.

"Who are those people anyway? There's so much fire...They can't be from The Necropolis, can they?"

The Necropolis. The domain of Darkness ruled by the Goddess Nimwae. We were attacked by Necropolis quite a lot, being The Sacred Land, the domain of light. But these weren't Necropolitan soldiers, I was sure of it.

"No, Levi. The attackers aren't Necropolitan."

"What about Lavasteam? Or Hell's Underground?"

I paused for a moment, thinking. The Goddess of Lavasteam was very good friends with the God of The Sacred Land – they had no quarrels. And Hell's Underground was far too weak to have an army like this.

"No, Levi. I don't think they are."

"Well? What are they?"

31

I studied a few soldiers I saw from a distance. I knew instantly they weren't from The Netherworld – They were unlike anything I'd ever seen. Their hair and eyes, so flat and dull and grey. Their skin, so bright in comparison, it almost shone like neon compared to our grey-ish toned skin. Their ears were unnaturally round and small unlike our long, pointed ears. A small gasp escaped my lips in realization. Was it possible?

"Enyo? Who are they?"

"Levi?" I asked patiently, calmly, "Answer very truthfully. Do you believe in humans?"

"Hu...h-humans?"

Everyone in Netherworld had heard of humans, even if seldom spoke of them; these creatures, supposedly living in a world parallel to ours. Rumours, scary stories, often told on summer and winter solstices to scare the young children, were told about times when the fine seam holding our two worlds together ripped. Just for a few hours, humans and Akoi could travel freely between the two worlds. Could it be true? Were the humans waging war on the Netherworld?

"I...I thought they were just a myth..."

"Well, apparently not. It seems that- ARRGH!"

Fire! I knew I had waited too long, the wall was on fire! Sparks raining down on us, the heat threatening to smoulder our flesh if we didn't move, move now! I grabbed Levi's hand and pelted through the city, not having enough time to strap him to my back. Quick! I had to hurry, go faster, I was in full view! The humans! Could they see me? Were they trying to shoot? I couldn't see. Everywhere was black and red with fire and smoke and blood. I knew the shelter was no longer an option. I had to get out of The Sacred Land altogether.

First left, then right, left, left again! Did I know the route somewhere deep in my brain, or was I just following my instincts? I had no idea, but it was as good guess as any. I could see a clearing in the smoke! A train to Airin! We were saved, if we could just get to that train! I ran faster, struggling through the flames! We were saved, we were gonna make it, we were...

"Gotcha!"

A sharp tug on my scalp, and I had been pulled to a standstill.

"Get off me, get off!" I fought, struggled, but the hand had a firm grip on my hair now.

"You're not going anywhere, red eyed demon," the human man snarled at me. I looked desperately around for Levi.

"LEVI!"

Another man had grabbed him by the shoulder, and he was fighting to get off, but with no success – The man was more than twice his size, and had a gun. Were we doomed? Was this the end? The man tugged at my hair again, making me wince. "Answer my questions!"

I stayed silent, defiant, glaring at him with all the hatred in the world.

"Where are we? Where is this place?"

Instead of answering, I worked up a mouthful or saliva and spat right in his face. He snarled, and hit me across the face sharply.

"You will answer me, or I'll kill your little friend here, right in front of your eyes!"

I stayed silent. Most of my defiance gone, replaced by fear. I stopped for a second, and then spoke. "This is The Sacred Land. It's one of the ten domains in the Netherworld."

"The Netherworld, eh? That's what you call this place? So, how did we manage to get here?"

I winced as his gripped tighter on my hair. "Your guess is as good as mine."

I needed to get out. My gun! I had left it behind the wall! I mentally cursed, not wanting to say any more than necessary. I had a knife in my pocket, but how could I escape with just a knife? Unless...?

I'm not sure how I did it. Lightning fast, I guess. Before I even realised what I was doing, the knife was out my pocket and I slashed across the back of my hair. Next thing I was holding Levi and we were running for the train.

I managed to grab onto the side of the train just before it left. Pulling open the doors I tumbled inside, still clutching Levi's small sweaty hand. I lifted a hand to the back of my head, anxiously feeling my now short hair. It was chin length some places, ear length others, some places still down to my hip, like it used to be. But I was alive. We were both alive. We were going to Airin!

I took a deep breath, and sunk back against the seat. We would be fine. The Netherworld Gods were strong. They would fight back. Make the humans pay!

I wrapped my arms around Levi, and fell into a deep, blissful sleep, lulled by the rhythmic rumbling of the train. We were going to Airin, and we would be okay.

I never have been able to get over that thick, sick feeling when I see a human. I never did recover my ability to love and trust fully. For most, that war was a horrifying experience, granted, but nothing more. It was over for them when the war ended. For me, the memories live on, burned into my mind and heart so deep I know that no matter how long I live, I will never forget them fully. One more minute in the Sacred Land and I'd have been dead. I didn't know what the war was about. It didn't matter. It didn't solve anything.

Wars never do.

By Sasha Kowal

CIRCUS

The town of Saulli was a relatively peaceful one. It wasn't a large town, more of a village; it had no more than two-hundred residents, and whilst that meant that the townsfolk were at ease with one another, it also meant that everyone knew each other's business. However, not one of them could have predicted the event that changed them all forever, the event that horribly dwindled the town's numbers. It all started when the circus came to town.

Asha Kennedy had rushed home from school on September the seventh. It was a strange sight, because she was normally a very discreet and reserved young lady, but on that day she tore through the streets like there was a monster on her heels.

Asha was racing through the town for one reason alone: a leaflet that had come through her letter box that very morning It was a most peculiar leaflet: it was circular and made of thick paper, with one side decorated with beautiful and mesmerising red swirls. On the other side it had a message, that read:

"One and all. You are welcomed to attend Vaughn's travelling circus, in town for one night only. It will be the night of your life."

Everyone in Saulli had received one, and whenever Asha and her fellow students in the town's very small school had a spare moment, it was all they could talk about.

"I've heard they've got tigers," Jane, the youngest pupil said with wide and eager eyes. "The tent's huge!" Rian had said, almost bouncing with anticipation.

"It's right on top of Briar's Hill!"

"We *know*," Daquan spoke up, and rolled his eyes. He and Asha were the oldest in the class and the only ones not trembling with enthusiasm. However, Asha was excited inside, while it seemed as though Daquan couldn't care less.

When Asha reached her house, she crashed through the door with jubilation. "Mother? Father?" she shouted, looking through the door of the empty living room.

35

"In here, love!" she heard her mother's reply from the kitchen.

Asha skipped down the hallway and slipped into the kitchen. "Afternoon dear," her father mumbled, not looking up from the newspaper he was reading. Her mother smiled up at her from the book she had been examining, and raised her glasses from her nose to balance on her temples.

"So," Asha sat down at the round table with her parents, the late afternoon sunlight casting a warm glow around the room. She placed her palms down onto the table, with the air of a business man about to pitch an offer.

"We are going to this circus thing, aren't we?"

"I don't know Ash," her father answered, putting down the newspaper and pinching the bridge of his nose. "I'm not feeling too well...it's been a long day at work..."

"Oh please can we go?" she interrupted, clasping her hands together and batting her eyelids furiously.

"A once in a lifetime experience...one night only," Asha's voice took on a higher tone of urgency.

"And everyone's going, literally the whole of Saulli...and I've been so good this year! I deserve to go, don't I, mother?"

Her mother had returned to her book, unwilling to get into this debate between husband and daughter. Her father sighed, and Asha's head whipped around to look at him.

"Fine," he said, resignedly, "we'll go to this circus thing if it means so much to you."

Asha squealed and shot up from the table to hug her father's neck. Her repeated "thank yous" could still be heard even as she left the room and trooped up the stairs to get ready.

"That girl's got you wrapped around her little finger," Asha's mother tutted, but she was smiling. Her husband chuckled as he picked up his paper again. "I know."

After Asha and her parents had changed clothes, they started off out of the door and started on their way to Vaughn's travelling circus. As if in sync, as they crossed over the threshold, they noticed all the other villagers were on their way to the circus at exactly the same time. Although that may seem strange to you, because all the villagers knew each other so well, they often did things at the same times coincidentally. So, all the villagers, including Asha and her family, set off on the way to Briar's Hill.

Briar's Hill was named so because the name who had founded Saulli was named John Briar. There was a little plaque on the door of the town hall saying so.

As the villagers walked as one up the hill, Asha admired the scenery. It was picturesque, with pink and orange evening skies, fluffy clouds and lush emerald coloured grass. Contented birds were cheeping their song, and the children of the village were falling behind and picking daisies. It could not have been a more perfect scene.

Soon the huge circus tent loomed into view and cast a dark shadow over the merry group. Asha couldn't help but notice that the colours were two very strange ones to be together; orange and purple. They made the tent look even more exotic and even hinted at danger.

There was not just the tent at the top of Briar Hill; there were also gypsy carts and trailers. Jane, the young student, looked around in vain for any sign of a tiger. The only animals outside the tent were the pretty tan horses that pulled the carts.

Asha noticed that despite earlier acting as if the circus was no big deal to him, Daquan had turned up too, with his family in tow.

The entrance to the tent was a flap which could fit through one person at a time. The villagers formed as steady queue to the entrance. They were not like city people, who were brash and rude; they were quiet and polite folk.

There was a person sitting on a chair on the left of the entrance, who was dressed very smartly in a top hat and a tailcoat. When Asha reached him (at least she assumed he was a man), the corners of his mouth turned up into a sinister grin that sent shivers running down her spine. He tilted his chin upwards, and under the brim of his hat, Asha saw a flash of yellow eyes.

Asha froze where she stood, paralyzed by fear and it was only a gentle poke in the back from her mother that spurred her into motion again, moving past the creepy man and into the tent.

Inside, the tent was lit only by the light coming in through a hole in the top and the currently open entrance.

There were tiered seats around the edge of the tent, making a circular performance area in the middle. Asha noticed how the performers must have worn away the grass in the middle quite quickly, since it was just dirt now.

The villagers barely took up half of the seats and they all sat together in one part of the seating area, leaving the other half dark and solitary. They spoke quietly but with excited voices, eager for the show to start. Once they were all seated, it began.

In the middle of the circle, a ring of fire lit up without warning. Captivated, Asha stared as the flames blazed in a perfect loop. Seemingly from the ring of fire, two eerie looking clowns appeared wearing colourful noses and speeding around on miniature bicycles. However, something made it more scary than amusing, especially when one clown fell over and started to cry tears of blood. A child screamed!

Then, with a honk of their noses, they were gone; vanished completely, and the audience gasped in awe. Before they even had time to clap, the villagers saw a new act take to the ring. Seven beautiful, thoroughbred horses with shining silver manes and tales trotted into the ring. At the front of the group, a girl of around Asha's age rode the most spectacular of the horses as if it was a part of her own body.

The horse followed her every whispered command, as did the others in their impressive feathered headgear. The lead horse even managed to stand on its hind legs without throwing her off. Asha and every other audience member were entranced by the act, and they gasped and clapped animatedly, whatever happened. Soon, much to their disappointment, the act ended, and the horses cantered out, whilst the next performer entered. A very short and beefy man, with a long twisted black moustache and bulging muscles that looked far too big on his small body entered the arena.

As he approached the ring of fire, Asha saw two weights appear that hadn't been there moments before; they were twice the size of the man's head. His meaty hands clasped around the bar of the weights, and he lifted it with ease. The strongest men in the village were put to shame when he pulled the weights off of the bar and started to juggle them.

The show kept getting better. After the beefy man, there were the most amazing dancers, a silent magician who could walk on water and even a magnificent silver lion, whose roar made the earth quake. Then, the tent seemed to get darker and creepier. The ring of fire continued to blaze, but the flames were even stronger now, burning blue. A young man appeared from within the ring of fire. He could have only been a year or so older than Asha, seventeen at the most. He had a strong jaw, pure white shoulder length hair and had defiant look about him. Unlike the other performers, who had lingered in the middle of the ring, he approached the audience, his strides long and confident.

"I need a volunteer," he said, looking into the faces of the villagers, and over the young children raising their hands hopefully. His eyes fell on Asha, and a sly grin spread across his lips. He pointed to her. "You!"

Asha merely blinked. She glanced behind her, only to find an elderly couple staring back at her. Her eyes slid onto the boy again and he grinned wider, beckoning her with his hand. So she stood up and made her way to the steps leading down into the ring. *"Why me?"* she thought, her heart pounding.

As soon as she stepped into the ring, the boy moved closer and took her hand.

"I hope you're not afraid of heights," he laughed quietly. Suddenly, the ring of fire spread out towards them and they were caught up in its fiery grasp. Asha screamed, terrified, and struggled to get away, but the boy held her hand very tightly, holding her there. Then the flames died down and, although she wasn't harmed in any way, Asha screamed again. She was in the middle of a tightrope which definitely hadn't been there before. Her blood ran cold in fear and she stayed completely still.

"It's all right," the boy whispered in her ear, "you won't be hurt."

Down below, the villagers yelled, and Asha looked down, horrified. Her parents, her friends, her neighbours, everyone was being taken away, put into cramped crates pulled by winged people and people with the bodies of horses.

When she looked up at the boy again she noticed his ears were on top of his head, and they were not human. They should have belonged to an animal, a leopard. Asha noticed his tail next, long and twisting. She screamed again and again, the boy laughed, a cruel sound that made the hairs on the back of her neck stand up.

"You only see us as we truly are when the show is over," he explained, showing a flash of sharp teeth.

"Welcome to Vaughn's travelling circus where the acts are human animal hybrids. I am Fabian, and, Asha Kennedy, you're one of us now."

By Tilly Wallace

GEMINI

"Tell us. Tell us what happened."

I looked up into the full glare of the lights.

"Tell us the whole story."

I stared at them, unsmiling. I took a deep breath and the policemen bent over their notebooks.

"It all started the day when the letter came."

The doorbell rang. I ran down the stairs and opened the front door. Haris was standing there. I smiled. We were next door neighbours and best friends ever since he came to live with Peter and Heather, his foster carers. He had a grim expression. Something was wrong.

"So what was wrong?" questioned the police man, bearing down at me.

"He took me to his place where his carers were waiting," I said, flatly, "they've received a letter. They've lost their jobs, been made redundant and can't afford to keep Haris anymore so he's going to be sent to a care home on the Isle of Wight. Someplace called The Gemini."

The Police looked at each other briefly and nodded once. Turning back to me, they smiled kindly. "Please continue with your story," they said.

I sat on the kerb watching the Police car drive away. I daren't linger there for long or I would never leave.

Two weeks later. The sea breeze blew in my face as I waited impatiently to board the ferry. It had been two weeks since he had had left but I hadn't heard anything from Haris, which was unusual. Haris Jones was well known for socialising on the net...Email, Facebook and Twitter...but he had gone quiet. Overnight I had made a rash decision to find him and booked a one way ticket on my laptop. I packed a bag with essentials and left the house in the morning, my parents assumed I was going to school but I took the bus to the port. There was one hour until I could board the ferry but it felt like a year.

"So you got onto a ferry to find answers?" said the policemen, disapproval lining their faces.

"Yes," I replied calmly.

"You didn't tell your parents?"

"I left them a note," I said as they tutted. I continued. "That was the least of my worries. I didn't know the trouble I was heading for.

The ferry docked in the Isle of Wight at half past eleven that morning. As I disembarked I scanned the empty beaches in the hope I would find him there. It was quiet, almost unnaturally quiet. It may not be the busiest season on the little island, but it was deserted apart from a group of people by the rock pools. I glanced over them, but I stopped and looked back. One of them looked familiar. I squinted at the group. It couldn't be... It was too much of a coincidence. It looked like Haris. I started to sprint towards them, tripping once or twice on the uneven rocks. When I got close, I began shouting his name.

"HARIS!"

He couldn't hear me. I shouted even louder, almost losing my voice in the process.

"HARIS! HARIS"

I was shouting into his face now but he didn't take any notice. The other children around stared at me. I ignored them. His eyes were glazed over and a vacant expression was plastered on his face. I wrenched the bucket out of his hand, marched over to the cold sea and filled it to the brim, then ran back and sloshed the water all over him, drenching him. He jerked and spluttered and rubbed his eyes and expelled a spout of water. He shook his head and looked up. His eyes widened.

"Helena? What are you doing here?"

"To rescue you of course," I replied and pulled him across the beach.

"But Castor will kill me if I leave. He's evil!"

"Oh come on. Doesn't matter about him! We'll get on the ferry!"

"You don't understand..." he started to say, but I just tugged at him even more and we approached the ferry. We squeezed through a group of backpackers and walked out onto the deck. However, someone was already there and Haris gasped.

"It's him Helena! It's Castor!" he hissed into my ear. He turned around and smiled at us and put his hand up in a casual salute. He was tall with a face that looked as though it was sculpted from marble and bore the mark of an arrow across his cheek. His smile was cold and frozen, his hair dark as night.

"Don't look so surprised," he said icily, "there are many things to catch."

He pulled out a bow and arrow out from nowhere and shot several seagulls down; they fell into the sea with a splash. He inspected the waters. I gasped and looked around to see if anyone was there but it was deserted. He turned to face us.

"So, Haris, who is your little friend? I don't recall seeing her around." His tone was light and conversational, almost pleasant, but his eyes were hard and narrowed. "Someone trying to help you is it? It seems to me you're trying to escape," he smiled coldly, "but that can't happen because nobody leaves Gemini. At Gemini we care for those without a home."

"Really?" I said angrily. "What are you really up to? All of those children," I pointed to the queue waiting for the ferry, "They're oblivious to the world...it's as though... as though you've drugged them!"

He laughed; a maniacal sound that made the hairs on the back of my neck stand up.

"You're not as dumb as I thought you were!!" he said, looking coldly into my eyes, "Gemini was set up so children could grow up to be....useful. They're apprentices of sorts. We choose orphans because no one cares for them."

I looked at Haris. His eyes narrowed and his jaw clenched.

"NO!" he said quietly. Castor glared at him. "People do care for me. Helena does. My foster carers did. I'm not going to Gemini. You're training kids to grow up to be something wrong.

You've drugged them! You drugged me…but you're never going to do that to me again!"

There was a moment of menacing silence as Castor surveyed Haris then again, he smiled.

"So you refuse to come with me even though you are not loved. It seems we're going to have to go with Plan B. You see I simply can't have you blabbing my secrets everywhere and the same goes for you missy," he said looking at me. "No one should live just because of care and love and what I see in front of me is a perfect example of what I'm trying to obliterate. Say goodbye you two. You'll probably never get off this ferry let alone feel dry land again." He advanced, his mouth twisted into a scowl.

We backed up against the railing. The ferry was already moving. He charged. I dived out of the way but Haris wasn't quick enough and he went over the railing as Castor slammed into him. I screamed for him. He turned to me, shaking his head.

"What a shame, he would have been a great leader. But you're the one to blame for his death, the same person who wanted to convince him of care and love." He put his hands around my neck and lifted me up. I gasped wildly struggling for breath as he hoisted me up over the railing. Spots flashed in my eyes.

"Any last words?

I croaked faintly and he dropped me over the railing.

I reached out frantically and my hand caught the railing. I heard a snarl from above amongst the panicking crowd. Castor yelled along with them. "You may take me, but the Gemini will still live on!!!"

I didn't have time to think about what he said. My head was still reeling from lack of oxygen and I felt a dam break inside of me as I thought of Haris. I started crying as my fingers slipped.

"HELP!" I cried, choking on my own words. A hand caught mine just as I fainted.

I was taken back to Plymouth and hauled into a police station. I was still crying because Haris was gone…all because of me.

"So that's it," I said, "the whole story."

The police men nodded at me sympathetically. "It will be alright Helena. Castor has been locked up. You will never have to see him again. And as for Haris," the policeman paused and cleared his throat, "we are extremely sorry but we will try and recover his body."

I nodded, looked down and bit my lip.

"You may go Helena."

I got up silently and went outside. It was raining. I pulled my hood up. I kept my head down. The news had travelled like wildfire through Plymouth and now everyone was trying to discern their own version of events. I scowled at the ground and kicked the kerb. I heard footsteps behind me and I looked up. I gasped. It was Castor. But it couldn't be. He was locked up and there was no arrow. I froze as the figure came closer. The expression was of absolute loathing. I started to back away, stumbling. The figure came and grabbed the front of my hoodie.

"This is for my brother," he breathed, and he punched me in the head. I collapsed onto the ground. When I woke up, I thought I was back in the police station as the lights blinded me. But as I blinked slowly, I saw that I was in a hospital room, quiet except for the sound of the fan whirring above me. I shook my head to try and remember what had happened but a shock of pain ricocheted in my head. I winced and closed my eyes. Gemini, plans, Castor swam through my head. There was something gnawing in the back of my mind as though there was something I needed to know. I screwed my eyes up trying to think. Gemini.... What had I heard about Gemini? I thought back to a history lesson when I wasn't paying attention... something about the Gemini twins.....

YES! That was it. The Gemini twins Castor and Pollux...... I bit back a scream as I felt my pulse racing. That's what Castor had been shouting about. I suddenly felt very ill. The door opened. I held my breath but it was just the doctor. He looked at me and frowned.

"Are you alright? Because I thought I heard something."

"Yes, I'm alright," I said quickly without any real conviction.

"Mmmmm. Ok. You should rest. That is one nasty bump on your head."

Suddenly I just blurted everything out as I broke.

"He's going to kill me! Gemini... Haris... the twins... JUSTICE!" I yelled the last word out. The doctor looked alarmed.

"I think you're going to need a scan. You might have a concussion," he said, his eyebrows raised.

I shook my head. "No!!! You don't understand! Gemini has a plan, to rid the world of what we care about! We need to stop them!"

The doctor smiled gently. "There's no such thing. You need to go to sleep."

"But..." I stopped. It was clear that I was fighting a pointless battle. Who would believe this sort of thing from a hysterical fourteen year old girl? I sank back onto the pillows.

"That's it," said the doctor. "I'll send the nurse with some painkillers." He left. I stared at the blank white wall opposite me. Was anyone going to believe me? No. No adult would. I grimaced as I thought. I was going to have to take matters into my own hands. When I get out, I was going to do everything in my power to stop Gemini. I started to close my eyes, but something caught the corner of my vision. I looked at the curtains, my heart suddenly in my mouth. There was a shape moving behind it, and it most certainly looked as though it was carrying a bow and arrow...

By Yueh-Chia Lo

LIFE IS LIKE A FOUR LEAF CLOVER

Just three more days to go! Three more days until we go to Ireland to play football! Me, Shannon and the Clipfield Rangers. If we can win three cup finals and the league title then surely we can win a tournament. To us, winning a tournament is a walk in the park!

My name's Arran. Arran O'Shea. My friends call me Azzy for short. The lads at football call me "Golden Boots" but I don't know why. My best friend, Shannon Minton, calls me "Bonnie Ronnie" because where I come from bonnie means "Young Fair Maid" and I walk like a girl.

I've been playing football since I was six. I turned thirteen last week so I've played for seven years. I started off training with lads I didn't know on a Wednesday night. Then at eight, I signed for Robin Hood Boys for two years. Since then, I've played for two other teams, Linfield and the one I play for now, Clipfield Rangers, that's where Shan comes in.

Shan is my best friend and she has been since we first met and she always will be. She's a bit younger than me but we're both in year 8. We both go to Clipfield High; we're in different halves though but we always hang out together at break and lunch. We're like peas and carrots.

The two days after that flew by pretty quickly, thankfully. At school, I sat in my lessons staring out of the window daydreaming but it doesn't matter as I'm in the bottom set. I'm a bit of a thick stick really. When the final bell went on Friday, I was out of the school gates faster than Usain Bolt. I had a lot of packing to do so I had to be home quickly. The problem was, I didn't know what to pack. So I rang Shannon.

"Hello Bonnie Ronnie."

"Hello."

"You don't know what to pack, do you?" she knew me too well.

"You know me too well," I replied.

"Well, I've packed my kit, my brown chinos, shorts, all my checked shirts and my PJ's."

"Ok. Thanks!" I said.

So I took my green and white football kit proudly off the coat hanger and folded it up neatly and placed it into the suitcase along with my beige chinos and my navy blue and white stripy t-shirt. I also packed my Celtic pyjamas and my Celtic hoodie, t-shirt and joggers for night-time. As I was packing, I started to get really excited. But this time it was a different kind of excitement.

"Arran! Your tea's ready," Mam shouted.

Waiting for me on the circular table was a plump chicken drizzled in honey. Then on the side were some crispy roast potatoes, finely chopped carrots and parsnips, glorious mashed potato with Yorkshire puddings around the side. To top it off, it was covered in a thick coat of beef gravy! As I walked towards the table, my mouth started watering and I started dribbling all over my school tie.

"Do you want a bib?" my Dad laughed and everything went back to normal.

I sat at the table and started eating a roast potato when someone knocked on the door. It was Shannon. I'd only just started my dinner but at the same time I didn't want to send her away.

"Are you ok, you look a bit shook up?" my Mum asked.

"I'm ok, it's just a bit cold outside," she replied.

"So what's up?" I questioned.

"I can't go to Ireland," she sobbed.

"Why not?!" I was really worried now.

"There's no one to take me."

"We'll take you!"

"But it's not fair on you if you've got to take all your stuff and all my stuff," she argued.

"Have you seen the size of my car?" I asked.

"Are you sure?" Shan questioned.

"Yes!"

So that's what happened. As soon as I woke up I rang Shannon. For the first time ever, she was awake before me. I finished packing my things and then carried them downstairs. My stomach started to rumble so I made myself breakfast. When I'd eaten my breakfast I couldn't move but I had to sometime! Shannon was at the door!

She had all her things with her but she said there was something missing. She emptied her suitcase so we could work out what was missing. She'd got her pyjamas and her football kit, her chinos and her shirts, her shorts and her Celtic kit but even I knew there was something missing.

"My mobile!"

"What?" I asked.

"I've forgot my mobile," she laughed.

"Oh right! Back in a minute!" and I made my way to Shannon's.

When I got back I helped Shannon and Dad load the car. First my things and then Shannon's. Once we'd finished, Dad started the engine and off we went. Ireland here we come! We were really excited and we couldn't wait to see what the tournament would bring. As we drove to Ireland, my Mum fell asleep and so did Dad.

Finally, when we reached Ireland, as we had been sat in the car for more than two hours, my legs turned into jelly and when I tried to stand up I fell over. Shannon thought it was hilarious. Connor and Robbi, the McQueen twins, ran up to meet us and say hello. Connor and Robbi were identical so I had to take a minute to work out which one was which. After a while, I figured Connor was wearing shorts and Robbi was wearing jeans; the only shorts he wears are his football ones!

We went to where we were staying to unpack and settle in. The parents were in one house and all the team in another. There were only four beds so Shannon, Niall, Taylor and I shared a room but I don't know about the others. The rooms were massive and the beds were heavenly. We were having a great time.

That night, we all met at the bar for a meeting about the match tomorrow. We were playing against Linfield Boys and then if we got through to the semis, we'd play against Portadown Lads, Cliftonville Junior, Coleraine Clovers Green, Crusaders Boys Red, Glentoran or Ballymena United. This was going to be a tough tournament and we're all excited about it. Kick-off was at 9'o'clock so we've got to have an early night.

The next morning, the sun was shining brightly in the bright blue sky as it shot us with its scorching rays. We were woken by the sound of music being played in the manager's room so it obviously meant he wanted us to get up. There was a knock at the door so Taylor answered it. Without invitation, in came a man in a tuxedo wheeling a metal trolley. Looks like we had room service. When we'd finished eating, we got ready in our kits and went to the pitch.

The whistle blew and the game began! I started upfront with Niall and Shannon started right back. By half time, the score was 3-1 to us. Taylor had knocked one in with his head, Niall tapped one in with his right foot and Shannon volleyed one in before the ball hit the ground. The whistle blew again and we went into the second half. They had no chance now! The final whistle went and we'd beaten them 8-2! There's the three scored in the first half then Johnny from the opposition scored an own goal and I scored four! We're in the semis.

That night we had a blast. The adults got drunk, we got tired so we all went home and pretty much fell asleep straight away!

So in the semi-final we're playing Crusaders Boys Red. This is going to be a doddle! How they got through the qualifiers, I'll never know! The first whistle went and the game kicked off. We were playing so strong as a team that the world's strongest man couldn't break us apart. At half time, we had 6 goals to nil! I told you it would be a doddle! The ref blew his whistle and we were back! Shannon had played the other team off the park! At full time, we'd won 8-0 so now we're in the final! We celebrated all night and into the early hours! But it was not over yet! We've got another team to beat and so we've got to try!

As soon as the referee blew his silver whistle, you could see, from miles away, the dedication and concentration on each member of the team's face and that the entire team were putting their backs and their all into this game. This game was the most important game of the tournament and we knew we had to win it.

Shannon had the ball in a very dangerous position, we all thought she was about to score her second goal of the tournament but we were wrong. Someone from the opposing team came in two footed on her and took her down like she was a domino. They'd just given away a penalty by fouling our best player! Shannon gradually got back up and sorted herself out ready to take the penalty. She quickly glanced at the ground and what should she find but a celtic green four leaf clover staring up at her, she picked it up and held it tightly in her hand. It nestled itself in the palm of Shannon's hand as she took one last quick look before the referee blew his whistle once again. The crowd was silent as she took a run up. She hit the ball, it curled like a banana and we all thought it was going to go out wide when........GOAL!!!!!!!!! It flew silently into the back of the net, which was twice the size of us.

The keeper had no chance of saving it! It was one of the best penalties I'd ever seen. Shannon Minton, my best friend, had just scored an amazing penalty against the best keeper in the league! As the crowd applauded my amazing best friend, Shannon got ready for the ref to resume the game. From the minute the whistle went, we were back in the game. We were like a jigsaw puzzle, we get completed, they take us apart and we fall straight back into place. We were a jigsaw puzzle that was determined to be complete at least once more in the thirty one minutes left in this wonderful game. The ball was about to reach Shannon's feet once more when the half time whistle went so we made our way back to the changing rooms.

Once we'd all reached to changing rooms, Fish, the manager, had a few choice words of his own about the foul but other than that, he seemed really happy! We walked back out onto the pitch and carried on with the game like nothing had happened. Shannon passed the ball along the ground to Taylor, who made a cracking pass to Niall's feet, who crossed it into the penalty box, where it was met by my head and bounced into the net! We'd only just started the second half yet we had another goal already! We were on fire! If you listened close enough, I'm sure you can hear us sizzling. With just twenty minutes left, the opposition pulled a goal out of the bag but can they pull off another one? The twenty minutes flew by like a bird and with just five seconds left, Niall gently tapped the ball, which silently rolled along the ground, into the back of the net! He was our champion! Niall Cox was our champion!

We arrived to that match thinking we were going to lose but who won? US! We hadn't just surprised the crowd, we'd surprised ourselves!

Life is like a four leaf clover, full of luck and you never know what it'll bring!!

By Bryony Candlin

THREE HANDS OF FATE

He thought about it. That was all he seemed to do these days. Think about things...and stuff. There was always 'stuff'. Humans called everything they didn't know, 'stuff." But then they were very dumb indeed. 'Thing' was another example. His contemplations were interrupted – that also seemed to be happening annoyingly frequently.

"What are you doing here? May I have a feasible explanation?" The guard, (whose uniform was 3 sizes too big for him) staggered across the rickety floor, hands flailing, discreetly snatching an alcoholic beverage off the sideboard.

"Yes sir, erm...." 'Sir' shifted uneasily in his chair. "If it is grade 10 then I should be there right now."

Down in sunny Australia, a little boy surrounded by forests and extremely muddy puddles, with complete irrelevance to this story, was playing with his brother who, on the other hand, had complete and utter relevance. In fact, this story would not exist without him. Anyway, they were playing the serious business of armies and were immersed. Two ghostly figures flickered anonymously in the evening light. The boys could not see them gliding in the forest and promptly rest on a tree to watch.

"This is the threat? You're joking!" Exclaimed the more grandly dressed of the two. The boys were rolling on the clearing, covered in mud oozing out of the ground.

"Yes, this is the boy," he pointed to the one with blonde hair and a mud moustache.

"How then can it be that a mud-splattered eight year old cannot have a fate?!?" Yelled the grander one, his gold and red robes billowing in the sun.

"Well, all we know is that we just can't give him a fate..." His gruff, snarling voice did not match his exterior of blue velvet and white cascading curls set in a soft complexion amid gnarled facial features. As for the red robed "Sir", he had a high-pitched squeak and jet black hair with sharp ears and nose, defined pools of hazel eyes where souls had been seen. You could tell. He was Fate.

53

Fate clasped his hands together and crossed his legs in a meditating position, (very hard to do on a tree trunk). The blue robed man coughed gruffly.

"Shall I start at the beginning, Sir?"

"Please do."

"Very well. Ott..."

"Just one question..."he interrupted.

"Sir?"

"If this *is* the boy who claims to have cheated fate, then why have I never heard about it? Considering it could be the start of a universal crisis."

"Well...oh, I'd better start at the beginning."

Otto Pukes. Not the grandest of names, but there we are. Was he about to change the history of this universe by becoming the first being to defy Fate? With all children, we give them fate at birth; a fate that entwines with everyone else's and, in turn, makes the world go round, in I drifted, eight years ago, and went to the next boy on my fating list, Otto Pukes. The boy looked at me with dark pools for eyes...deep...quite like yours Sir. Fate flinched at this but waved a hand to indicate Paul should carry on.

I remember feeling taken aback. So shocked in fact, that I let my invisibility shield falter, I was sure they almost saw me so I popped the cork and his fate was given. Or so I thought. I hastily got back into the portal. Funny, it was as though those eyes could have seen right through me. The blue robed wizard faltered at this point, paused to savour the full impact his words should have. "Enough of theatrics, Paul," said Fate impatiently. "Get on with it."

Paul composed himself.

The next "Incident" was when he was five years old. There had been a failure in the works and it all pointed to him. We all presumed it was a blip. When I got there the same boy was simply holding a red bike, riding around to the shops. I checked my notes. "He should be riding a blue rickety old bike and consequently fall off, break his neck, arm and back in three places, dying in 48 hours." This problem needed to be rectified

54

immediately. A wide grin emerged on his face when he appeared from the shop holding an ice cream. He didn't look as if he was dying. I consulted my notes again. "He picks the bike on Tuesday, 27 July." This was Wednesday. After a time blip, (which involved a change of clothes) I strolled into the bike shop. There stood an adamant five-year old, pointing at the shining bike he would be riding tomorrow. I turned my invisibility shield off and spoke to the bike owner out of eye line of the boy and his greasy mother. It was easy to imitate him. Coming out of the dingy back room I greeted the mother and the troublesome five-year old.

"Which bike would you like lad, eh?" I have acquired good accents over the years.

"That one, that one!" the child yelled, stomping up and down. The barriers of fate were pushing the child so much already, I could feel it. How could he resist?

"Oh, Sonny," I replied, "that one is £50,000. I'm not sure you would want it." The mother sighed; she pointed to the shop window wearily. It read "Bikes for under £100" I grimaced.

"Idiot," Fate muttered under his breath. Paul ignored him.

"Of course we can do a special deal for, erm, toddlers." I can let this one slip, I thought. I would just have to kill him tomorrow. Then again, I had another thought about Fate. How could this boy, merely five years of age, challenge such a primal force? With such powerful intellect, this boy, if he was merely a boy...the thought struck me so strongly that I was forced to withdraw from the premises.

"We do not know what we are dealing with." And, with that thought thumping though my brain I backed away, terrified, from this *dangerous* child. I knew he needed to be killed. Or at least thrown into a cell where he couldn't ever be dangerous. Forever!

Paul pulled out a scroll, written in what appeared to be hurriedly scrawled ancient script, from the folds of his cloak. He read,

"*...As though the man hadn't got a clue what he was talking about and then this look of fear spread out over his face. He wen' away from my son at first, very slowly and cautiously to begin with*

*and then he jus' fled.... I mean, how rude!! I come in about buyin'
a bike for my son. I was willin' ta spen' a decent amoun' a money,
an' all he can do is be rude to me son!! Sandra? Ar' ya still
there?"*

An excerpt from a telephone call from Jane Pukes.

"I never liked her," admitted Fate, "although she was quite
funny at times..."

"You knew her?" Paul exclaimed, evidently surprised, but Fate
took no notice.

Fate stood up, his height unbelievably tall. "It means he brings
our downfall...it is prophesied...but not this soon. The situation is
grave." Paul nodded in acknowledgement and also rose. They
drifted away from the forest, leaving the two boys rampaging
through the greenery. They stepped though the portal, instantly
invisible. Gone.

As Fate and Paul passed through the Portal, Fate considered
the events of the past 48 hours. It puzzled him that he could not
find the missing fate. He had been searching the universe
through telepathy whilst Paul was talking but to no avail. It was
apparent that Otto didn't have his own fate, or destiny planned,
but when Paul tried to give him one, where did it go? He couldn't
have no fate, really. No one could do that except Fate himself.
And that is me, he thought giving a rather psychotic grin. No one
can compete with me and this little boy was a temporary
distraction.

Oh no, thought Paul, watching as the psychotic grin spread
across Fate's face as he rubbed his hands gleefully together. "This
is really getting to his head." The portal shuddered shut. Entering
the Council chambers, Fate burst in dramatically. Then he began.

"As you know, I have been away for a few days, on business
matters with Paul, my associate. He is busy elsewhere at the
moment but I was looking into the fate of a boy. As with all
children, he was given a fate at birth, but he has not allowed it.
The boy has diverted it in numerous ways and sees it as a game
and, in addition, I am unable to find his fate anywhere. But, no
fate can go missing, just like that. It has to glue itself to

56

something that hasn't got one already, which is nothing. It could very well be in another universe. I suggest our first action is to find the fate, put it back on the child and if all else fails, we lock him up forever." He then stopped to give the Council time to think. Then there was uproar.

"One at a time please!!" Fate bellowed.

Paul entered, a quarter of an hour later, to find the Council in deep discussion. Fate was in the depths of it all and it was clear they had come to a conclusion.

"Those in favour of finding the fate with the punishment death by charge?"

Nearly everyone stood up.

"Those in favour of finding the fate and setting the boy free?"

No one.

Fate announced, "In that case, find him!"

A few years later

Fate was extremely occupied examining the fate meter. Wait a minute... "controlthose blips, John!" Fate shouted down to the control room.

"There are no blips sir, there hasn't been for the past 48 hours," John's coarse voice yelled back to him.

"Then what is this?" There was a scurrying sound as John made his way up.

"Yes sir?"

"Look at this." John strolled over to the panel and creased his brows.

"Hold on a minute.....It's correct alright," Fate glanced hesitantly. "Are you sure?"

"Yep."

"It was suspected. No, it's not going to happen just yet."

Barely ten minutes later, Fate was summoned into his office. There lay a sack, wriggling helplessly on the table, it then fell off and started wriggling on the floor. It was just as he had ordered so why was he surprised? Fate stared at it the sack for some brief seconds then opened it. A teenager fell out, and stared at him.

Fate flinched and just as the boy was about to open his mouth, Fate put the tips of his fingers to his temples, the boy fainted. Fate kicked the body under the chair but he was too late; Paul thrust the door open. "Where have you been? I..."He broke off. The boy soon came round.

"Now," said Fate, "I am going to kill you little boy. It will ultimately seal my reign."

Otto stared at the insane man, who was now waltzing out the door. Paul edged towards the door and quickly fled. Fate returned and raised a doubled barrelled shot gun. The boy stood rooted to the spot, cemented into a penetrating stare.

"HAHAHAAAAA!" yelled Fate in a maddening tone. He lifted the gun up to nose height, aimed and fired. His finger caught on the trigger. He tried to press it down, but couldn't.

"It is *your* Fate *no*t to kill me," said the boy, in a monotone voice.

"Your time is old and done, and my turn has come".

The boy turned the gun to Fate's head, Fate powerless to stop him.

"You have been a capable and strong leader. I will strive to continue the course of fate, following in your footsteps.... Father. Even though I have no Fate, this one event I have no power over.

Goodbye."

And with that, Otto sent the bullet piercing through Fate's brain, dropped the gun and walked out.

by Tabitha Daniels

NEW BEGINNINGS

Chapter 1

LOGGED ON
BBI AMERICAN JAMES DARWIN
I'm in America now and I love it! It's about 44 degrees in Washington DC. Since it's January, usually I would have to wear coats in England, but not here. It's been my dream since I was 8 years old to come here. My mum and dad had to transfer country to start a new business because America is bigger, also, because England is already over populated with zoos.

I have a younger sister, Ashley, she's 8 and she's afraid of the dark. She mostly loves animals but hates lizards and spiders. She absolutely freaks out when she sees them, no matter what size they are. I'm James, I'm 12 and I LOVE ADVENTURES!

LOGGED OUT
"James! Can you get off your laptop and help out moving everything into Ashley's room!" Mum shouts, aggravated and annoyed.

"Coming!" I yell back. "I'm finishing off here." Mum can be so mardy when she's stressed and tired.

So I run excitedly downstairs to help finish off Ashley's room. The moving crew arrived the the day before us, so they placed all the main furniture in the house. The living room was quiet because everyone was outside apart from mum who was placing photo albums on the shelves. I sigh out loud. There is a lot to be done in Ashley's room with all her toys needing to be put away but she only has dolls, teddies, a dressing up kit and play babies. I wish I could go outside like everyone else but I'm the only person who hasn't done my listed job. Mum's doing the garden, living room and kitchen. Dad's doing the dining room, upstairs hallway and any other room and Ash is doing the hallway and near the front door.

After a few hours of Ashley changing her mind about where to put things in her bedroom, I collapse on the bed at about 10pm. Tomorrow is going to be a very long day. I fall asleep after 30 minutes of panicking about starting school.

On the way to school I start to go full scale panic. These kids are Americans and they'll probably be way cooler than me. I will be the English freak that's just moved here, is as pale as the clouds, 5 foot 2 skinny and underweight...with garnet coloured eyes. Almost everyone will have brown or blond hair too. Mine's unusually bronze and shaggy with a fringe that reaches to my eyebrows.

To make matters worse I'm not the popular type, you know, the above average type. I'm just an ordinary, friendly, chatty but pathetic English bloke. Everyone in the car is quiet this morning. The only noise is the car engine purring and Ashley sniffing and biting her nails. I know what she's crying about, everyone does. She misses Stella, our old family pet cat. She usually sits on Ashley's knee on the way to school, purring because she loves being in the car. Dad had to give her to our neighbour in England because I became allergic to cats and Ashley's never been the same now that she's not around anymore. She thinks it's my fault...I don't blame her.

The car engine cuts off and I realise that we're parked outside Ashley's school. We went to private schools in England because we were quite rich but mum and dad have to start at the bottom until they find enough money to open a zoo. I have to walk down the road to Boston High School. I was about to get out of the car, when dad breaks the silence, "Just be yourselves you two and...remember, they're still just people. Americans are really friendly and funny so try not to act like the odd one out." His voice goes quieter the more he speaks. Dad was bullied when he was at school and I feel bad for him. Mum steps slowly out of the car, shutting the door quietly. I grab my bag and get out quickly, I know I'm early but I want to get to the receptionist first.

Chapter 2, Horror Stories

I walk into my form room dazzled, it's huge! I've been gaping like a fish ever since I got to the front gate. You wouldn't think it's a school, you'd think it was a mansion! It's got a giant back field about 2 miles long, full of benches, sand pitches to play football and an outdoor canteen where they sell ice cream but it's closed now. The front of the school has black gates, about 3 metres tall and an automatic opening to a giant rectangular white building with a bright green lawn in front of it and a straight pavement that goes from the gate to steps that lead up to glass double doors that swing open automatically. It's like the schools you see on TV but better and bigger and brighter, irritably brighter! As soon as you walk through those doors, on your left is another set of these glass double doors that are labelled, 'Reception Area' where there are chairs and a semi-circular desk on the left side of the rectangular room.

Straight ahead I can see lockers and wooden doors with classroom numbers on them. I've been told my form room will be number 8. The Receptionist told me to wait in my form room until the bell goes as I don't know anybody. She also gave me a map. Dad was right, American people are really nice. My form room is about 7 metres long and 4 metres wide and painted orangey scarlet but the carpet is bright pale blue. Strange colour scheme! It has single white wooden desks, there are no double ones. On the wall at the front of the class is a blackboard. I take a seat on the second row in the middle line and look at my timetable again. First period I have Art with Mr Wright, then it's break-time and after that English with Mr Clark, Spanish with Mrs Vesse, then lunch. Also double DT with Miss Nutmeg (LOL). Then my form tutor walks in.

"What are you laughing at?" she asks kindly. I stare at her, politely. This day was going to be trouble free. I feel so confident and happy.

Nobody here is shy. They make you feel so alive and normal. Everyone in the form talked to me, well the boys anyway but I forgot most of their names as soon as they told me.

The only ones I can remember are a boy with chestnut brown coloured hair and blue eyes. His name's Zac and he seems very friendly and popular and then there's the girl who sits next to me, she's called Nicole and she's also very popular. She has long, straight gold hair and unusual dark amber pupils. She's kind of good looking but she's like me, average. She's only popular because her best friend is; at least that's what I've heard. All my classes so far are alike because Zac and Nicole are in all of them with lots of other people whose names I can't remember yet. The teachers all seem nice, not too strict or too kind.

At lunch Zac introduces me to his friends but I still can't remember all their names and I don't recognise any of them from my classes.

After we've got our lunch and found a table they explain to me about the parks nearby. Zac says, "Everyone calls it the haunted forest." I frown questioningly.

A blond haired boy says, "Yeah, many years ago a gipsy visited Boston Park, that's on Greenwood Lane, just around the corner and he brought a few animals he'd adopted. He walked along to the giant forest and when he saw a tree house, climbed up and left the animals there, then he walked back to the park because he forgotten his bags. The thing is, we didn't know the animals had leprosy, he did."

The boy became dramatic the more something new happens. His expression goes from neutral to completely horrified, white blank eyes and face. Zac continued the story with a bored expression like he's unimpressed because he's heard it enough times, "So, it starts thundering directly above the forest and forked lightning struck the tree. It caught fire right away. The gipsy charged back into the forest with a fire extinguisher he kept handy and stopped the fire from spreading but he was never found. Police searched but then even they couldn't be found so helicopters went over the forest and the pilot saw bodies lying on the ground but they were too far away to be able to identify them. They could see the animals running around the forest but they seemed to have lost their minds. Nobody ever went in that forest again. There are some people who don't believe the stories but are too scared to test it out. There was one teenage boy who didn't believe it and was stupid enough to go in there, his head held high and a dagger in each hand, but like everyone else, he never got back. Still, there are rumours that the animals are still there but went insane with hunger and fear of the fire and are breeding as we speak. People are saying in years to come the town will be overtaken with animals. That's if you believe in such things."

His voice held boredom but buried deep inside was disbelief and fear. I am shocked, shocked to my core. Mum and dad had never mentioned this. Maybe it's a joke? I ask in a small voice, "Are you guys joking?" My voice sounded raw, as though I've only just woken up. Nobody answered. They didn't have to. I could see in each every one of their faces that it was no lie. The five boys at the table have the perfect mirror expression of pale faces full of fear with blank eyes and I wonder if they realise they have all got their mouth opened shaped like an 'O'.

Only Zac kept a composed face, though he did betray the slightest bit of determination to test out the stories himself. Everyone's been quiet for a few minutes when I ask in a clear voice, trying to break the tension that's making me wonder if I look exactly like them, "so what were the animals, tiger a kangaroo... I don't know... a dog?"

A boy with dark brown hair, who I think is called Christ, says "Nobody knows.......the zoo researchers where he got the animals from can't gather all the information on which set of animals he brought. They were all young...babies and there were loads, panthers, crocodiles, werewolves and other animals nobody's ever heard of...." The boy's voice sounds like inside of a tomb.

The bell rings loudly. It makes all of us jump a mile out of our seats. It wakes us up and brings us back to reality. We started joking and laughing, back to the cheerful selves. The rest of the day was pretty boring, mainly because I did textiles in DT. One of Zac's friends who mainly hung around with the most popular girl of the school, walked with me and talked about how hilarious Miss Nutmeg was and how everyone always imitates her, not just because of her name. I also found out that she only talks about her children when it's not about textiles. Although I did have a bit of a laugh, I was on a dorky table so I wasn't exactly sure what was going on. Altogether, an average first day at a new school!

Chapter 3, The Truth

Mum and dad both turn around when I get in the back seat. Ashley glares at me, hmphh! Someone's down in the dumps. Mum asks impatiently, "So how was your first day at Boston? Made any friends? People nice?" It came out in such a rush it was hard to separate the words. I hesitate. "Everyone was curious about my life in England but I've made friends with the popular side and everyone's very nice."

Am I imagining the disappointment in her face? She just nods. Dad turns on the engine and then blurts out, "Did anyone tell you about the story called 'The Haunted'?" My instinct tells me to lie. Hopefully dad can't see my face. He's the only person who can tell by my face whether I'm lying or not. I look down and try not to do my lying habits that give me away. Like scratching my arm or losing eye contact. So I pretend to think about it then say, "No, it never came up, everyone was too busy asking questions about England." I shrug, trying to be casual. Careful not to breaking eye contact I ask, "Why is the story fake? Are you going to tell me about it?" Mum squints at me. She knows I'm lying but I didn't break eye contact! I looked at my face in the rear view mirror, its gone blue with fear and determination displayed on my face.

Then I realise I have been hiding the truth even from myself ever since I first heard it. I want to see if I can survive in the forest and I discover I'm hungry for adventure, because of my ordinary, dull English lifestyle in Rye. I nervously flick my fringe so it's covering my eyes. Mum then says, forcefully, "I was going to tell you myself, but if you don't believe it then that's fine…because I don't either."

Something was hidden deep behind her eyes. At the end of her sentence, it sounds as though mum has changed her opinion. Also, dad gives mum a quick dirty look as soon as she said she didn't believe it herself……strange. Ashley flicks her bronze ringlet curls that hang to her waist in my face and mum and dad turn their attention to the road. I made a promise that I'll talk to Ashley about her foul mood, since she only ever tells me what's wrong with her.

Chapter 4, Resistance?

I walk on Ashley's heels to her bedroom, so she can't hide and sit down front of her. She pretends to pour tea into my mini, plastic, posh, cup. I impatiently say, "thank you." Finally, she speaks, "Look J, haven't you ever thought that we're a bit different from dad. I mean LOOK, different?" she says irritably and softly. Her chocolate brown eyes stare miserably into mine. I was going to tell her she's talking nonsense but she stares at me and I see what's she's getting at. For instance, mum's eyes are the same colour as Ashley's, but dad's are blue and mine are green. We (me and Ashley) have bronze colour hair but dad's is brown and mum's is ginger red. Also, their hair is straight as a straw but ours…is curly? A tear trickles down her rosy cheeks from her right eye. She then says, "What if Phil is not our real dad?" Her voice breaks when she says the word 'REAL'. I budge over to her side and give her a tight hug. She starts weeping heavily on my shoulder.

I know how she feels. This is probably the first proper talk I've had with her since I became allergic to cats. I also can't believe I've never thought about it before. On top of all that, I just can't accept it until I talk to mum and get her to explain it all to me. I decide to rummage in mum and dad's room for clues, well evidence. I pat Ashley gently on her back and break away from her grip. I tell her I need to go downstairs so mum doesn't wonder what's going on. I watch her face carefully to check I haven't offended her and she nods at me I head out of her room and walk quickly downstairs. I'm not going to investigate right now, I guessed they were listening for noise because they weren't talking. Unless mum's cooking dinner, that is. I sniff. No. She's not.

Weeks have gone by, slow and painful. Slow because America is different with night and day than England. Painful, I'm always stuck on the same questions. Is Phil my real dad? Is 'The Haunted' story told exactly the same as what really happened, or is it a myth? Is mum hiding something because it has something to do with my real dad? Is that why dad gave her a dirty look? Is that why mum never answers questions when we ask something about our looks being different to theirs? So many questions need answering and explaining. I'd found no answers in mum's room.

In one week I'd be going to Lawrence's birthday party, he's one of Zac's best mates, on the 20th February. They said it was exactly the same day as the gipsy went to the haunted forest but I didn't want to get into that discussion again. That night I got undressed, had a bath, then slipped into bed and turned off my lamp and soon after I fell into a deep, deep sleep.

Chapter 5, Nightmares

I open my eyes. I see the tree house I've been trying to find. So far I've not died. Thankfully. The blazing hot sun burns the top of my head. I clench my spear tighter as I jump at a loud roar behind me. I spin around, pointing the spear straight forward to whatever is behind me. The lion displays its sharp fangs dripping saliva all over my head. The last thing I see is the lion pouncing on me, ripping my clothes apart.

I jolt upwards from my bed, heavily panting with sweat dripping down my face. This dream has been haunting me since last week. Always the same one, it never changes but even though I'm getting used to it, it still scares me. I get up and have a cool, then cold shower. The forecast is for 80 degrees today and I

66

think it's necessary. Today is Lawrence's birthday party. I decide to wear baggy jade green camouflage shorts with an orange sports shirt, see through tank top and brown flip flops. I take extra items like socks, trainers, black umbrella, parka with hood and, for emergencies my Blackberry Virgin phone. Also a few plasters and bug spray in case I get bitten or stung. I almost forget my sun cream and hat.

Chapter 6, The Adventure Begins
Ashley Darwin

James and I walk towards the beaming light, yellow meadow, where the party is held. Lawrence invited me too, since we became friends. I wear a turquoise flower dress that flows when I move and I've got a shoulder bag to hold my sun cream, red shorts, white silk tank top with white socks and trainers and I've got a red hoodie and an umbrella.

It has been exactly half an hour since we arrived and the party is a blast! I hung around with a girl named Nicole, because the rest were boys. Nicole said her friend couldn't come so she thought she would be the only girl. I thought Nicole was very pretty. When I tell her she answers, "Nah, you're prettier. You're very mature for your age, you know." I'm flattered so I say, "Thanks, you're quite mature yourself," she nods and we go quiet for a while. Then she says very quietly, "You're my mini me," we both laugh out loud.

Suddenly a giant blue butterfly lands on my knee. I gasp. Then it flew away. NO! I stood up quickly and sprinted after it. I could hear Nicole shouting after me and following. I was close enough to see where it was going. It flew out of the bottom meadow gate and out to a sandy pavement that lead to a dark overgrown forest. It looked like a horror movie. I stopped at the end meadow gate.

A strong cold wind came from the right and blew the hair over my face. It gave me goose bumps. At that exact moment the sun broke through the clouds and made the meadow turn from too bright to dark red. Sunset! I yanked off my flip flops and popped on my trainers.

I already put on my top and shorts under my dress. Nicole is just a few feet away from me, walking. Then I remembered the butterfly and searched frantically. I saw it and sighed in relief. It was on the branch of a tree that stood beside an overgrown trail leading into the forest. Nicole screamed in horror for me not to walk anywhere near the forest. I rolled my eyes at her. Jeez, she's worse than mum. The butterfly fled into the forest and I charged faster than the wind into the forest after it. Nicole screamed so loudly it bounced off the trees. She sprinted after me, breathless as she screamed, "No! It's the Haunted Forest! Don't go in there. You'll die!"

"What?" I didn't stop running. I remember mum mentioning it on the first day of school. I was too upset to ask more at the time, and forgot about it afterwards. I carried on and broke through the trees after the butterfly. It looks much scarier here. The butterfly flew between an oak tree and a tall tree I've never seen before and I realised I have left the main trail. Oh well. I stepped through a bush. Wow!

Chapter 7, Trouble
James Darwin

At sunset, everyone was starting to eat after all the dancing. Then I realised that the two girls were nowhere in sight. I stared at the bottom meadow gate. I could only just see Nicole's back as something echoes off the trees but the music's a bit too loud for me to make out what it is. I headed towards the sound.

John asked, "Where're you going?" I stared at him curiously, I wondered if he was going to spread another rumour about me.

"To the meadow gate, I am going to get Nicole and my sister," I say slowly...John's party whistle fell out of his mouth and he gasped, his face full of fear.

I wondered if this was a prank. Chris overheard and shouted so loud all of Zac's mate's turn around to listen.

"You've got to be kidding! That leads to the haunted forest!" Oh no! My head was spinning and I felt faint but I sprinted to the bottom of the meadow, ignoring all the yells of fear and warning. Zac followed after me, he didn't speak but just ran with me for a short while then, breathlessly he said, "I'm coming with you...but...how you are going to find them? I know Nicole would never go in there willingly, she was probably chasing Ash."

"Just follow the butterflies," I said so seriously he knew I wasn't joking. He didn't ask anymore because maybe he knew Ashley would chase them. We passed through the meadow gate. Neither of us spoke as we crept closer and closer to the forest.

Chapter 8, Trapped
Ashley Darwin

I'm lost. I've lost Nicole or Nicole's lost me. I've been here for about five minutes now and it seems that the forest is shivering and dancing in the wind. It's much darker. I was squashed inside my hoodie with my arms crossed walking fast, breathlessly. The trees are all bent over like a cave-mouth and it's hard to see the sky. The forest floor is overgrown in places with grass that's up to my shoulders. I stop at a muddy patch that's perfectly smooth and dry.

I shrug it off and continue to walk over it but, as my feet met the square patch of dirt, it bent inwards and then collapsed. I screamed as I felt myself falling. It wasn't a pleasant feeling. I was scared.

The falling made me dizzy and weary. Like when you fall off your bed and it scares you because you didn't see it coming. This is a hundred times worse. This is the longest fall I've ever had and then I landed, splash, into a swampy puddle. The force of the water knocked my breath out of me. The filthy water floated me to the top after falling back first, eyes shut tight.

Someone pulled me out onto the muddy ground as I coughed out dirt and water. I tried to open my eyes but the mud glued it together. Then I felt someone wiping my eyes. After I was free of dirt and blindness I opened my eyes and looked into a concerned pair of green eyes.

Chapter 9, The Truth in Animals

At first I thought it was James, but it wasn't. This stranger has dark, bronze, curly hair to his chin. That's why I'd thought it was James, and then I saw it was a man. The first thing I wondered was why anyone would be in the forest, the second thought was I needed to find out what happened in the story.

So I ask him, "Everyone is talking about a horror story called 'The Haunted'. Could you tell me this story and how you got in here?" The man nodded and explained it all in an English accent. When he got to the end he said, "I'm the gipsy," in a proud voice.

My anger flared. I asked him, "This is entirely your fault, what were you thinking?!" I frantically struggled to stand up but the man stared at me in confusion. Then he answered, "That's what people believe but it's not true. The real story is that I was a travelling gipsy but couldn't tell the woman I loved. She got pregnant and I had to tell her the truth. When I was leaving I told her, if she had a son, to name him James. That's it really."

JAMES?! I shrugged it off as a coincidence. The gipsy continued, "A few years later I went to check on her. She told me her husband couldn't have children so she needed me to make another child. Some time later I came to America to study animals and found out that only gifted children can hear animals, can speak to them all their lives. So I bought a lion, baby tigers and bears. I did some practice, then I realised I could hear them but not as clearly as I used to when I was a child. So I bought some animals, males and females, secretly, to make a zoo without any distractions and without anyone knowing. Sadly, the animals I bought were sick and needed children to spread the news for them. But then the only boy who came in wasn't gifted so he just went to another part of the forest and decided to camp there. But my children are destined to make things right, they are the

Chosen Ones. "The animals told me you fell into the cave, so I came to help you. What's your name?"

I was gobsmacked. Animals can speak to humans! The Chosen Ones! I whisper, "Ashley Darwin."

Chapter 10, Confessions

The gipsy stared at me, his expression a picture of success and joy. Then he sang out, "You're my child...or one of them!" I gasped really loudly. He calmed down and spoke more gently but cheerfully, "Look, your mum and stepdad were going to tell you when you reached twelve, and..."

"You don't have to explain I understand, I found out about it on my own. So, I can talk to animals? That's cool. Well, sign me up. Take me to your animal friends and I'll ride 'em to my brother and then I can take them to my parents, who are trying to set up a zoo. They already know about this talent we have don't they?" He nodded, trying to control his joy.

Chapter 11, Mission Accomplished

The lion's coat felt soft and smooth as I rode him and he kept telling me knock, knock jokes. He was hilarious! He also told me that the tigers had already gone ahead to find my brother and Nicole and my real dad had gone to talk to my parents about the zoo and working together.

As we turned around the corner I firstly saw Zac and then James and I explained EVERYTHING to them. So they're both standing there, looking like they want to whoop in relief that it's all over.

When we all finally found Nicole she ran to James, petrified until she had heard it all explained and then we all headed back to the meadow to get fences for the zoo. Some of the animals had built a tunnel to go underground so that's all sorted and we then went off together to find the animals what were still trapped in the forest. Mum and dad understood everything and they were as relieved as everyone else that all the stressful secrecy was over.

Chapter 12, The Happily Ever After
Logged on

BBI, AMERICAN James Darwin
So, six months later everything has changed. Mum and dad have opened a worldwide zoo and people everywhere want to visit the zoo because of its history. Within those six months they have taken on seventy four zoo workers, all the trees in the forest have been chopped down to build pens and homes for the animals and the zoo was built where the forest was.   Nicole is helping me to tell the story of us going in to a forest that people believed had crazy animals and then finding out that it was not true. Ashley looked after all the cat family and she forgave me my allergy to cats. Also, we moved house next door to the zoo and everyone moved on with their life.

Logged out

By Jemima McKenzie

Group Three

Secondary School

Years Nine and Ten

MRS HAWSHORE WAS BORING

Mrs Hawshore was boring. Her dull clothes were boring, her lifeless face was boring, her monotonous voice was boring...there wasn't one thing about her that wasn't boring.

Every year, the children who had chosen biology scanned their timetables to see which teacher they'd been given. Half would throw their timetables up in the air, grinning. The other half would scowl, let their timetables drop to the floor and cup their head in their hands.

It was this half who had been given Mrs Hawshore.

There was only one thing that was interesting about Mrs Hawshore's classes. This was the real human skeleton which stood in the corner of the room. For decades this had been the only thing which entertained the poor victims of Mrs Hawshore's classes, and David King and Lewis Smith were no exception to this.

The two boys had been best friends for as long as they could remember and were famous for being trouble makers. Any teacher would have ensured immediately that these boys were not seated next to each other, but Mrs Hawshore paid such little attention to her class that she'd hardly realised they were even in it. Each lesson, the boys would amble in, a little later than the rest of their class and plonk themselves down in two seats, as close to the back as they could.

Now, Mrs Hawshore's lessons were generally so boring that even the naughtiest of children weren't bothered about trying to ruin them. However, David and Lewis really were something else.

At first, the things they did were so minor they were hardly noticed. For example, when Mrs Hawshore left her chair to write on the board, they would leap up from their seats and change the page of the text book she read from daily. But Mrs Hawshore simply sighed and changed it back. After a few weeks of this David and Lewis grew bored, as did the rest of the class. They were tired of seeing the same trick, lesson after lesson, and were somewhat disappointed not to have yet witnessed one of the legendary David-Lewis practical jokes.

The boys needed to do something really spectacular, but a few weeks passed and they could think of nothing. It seemed as though there was nothing in the dreary room that could inspire one of their famous pranks. What they didn't realise was that there was one thing in the classroom which could kick up a stink that would go down in history.

It was just a normal day. The boys were late after being reprimanded in the corridor for tying a first-year's shoe laces together. As they neared the room, they were still laughing about the way the poor boy had tripped, head over heels.

"Sit down." Mrs Hawshore's voice boomed as they opened the door. They glanced towards their usual places at the back but they were taken, leaving only two places in the corner...the skeleton corner. Still laughing, Lewis sat down first leaving David to sit on the end. As he slumped down, David's satchel caught the shinbone of the skeleton, causing it to wobble slightly before becoming stationary again. The movement was barely noticeable to the rest of the class. A bang or a shake from David's direction was nothing out of the ordinary.

David realised something wasn't quite right and, glancing up from his desk, he soon realised what. Mrs Hawshore - who was only seen moving if she was travelling from the staff room to her classroom - was out of her seat. She was leaning on her desk for support, with her palms placed either side of the closed book. Her grey face was spiked with pink and her eyes were blazing with a wave of fury.

The abnormality of the situation hit David like a ton of bricks and he felt as if his feet had been plastered to the floor. Mrs Hawshore and David stood, staring into each other's eyes, for what seemed like an age. Beneath his un-tucked school shirt, David's heart was racing. Beneath her pristine, creaseless blouse, Mrs Hawshore's heart remained as still as the rest of her body, as if she had been encased in stone. Tension hung in the air like an unwanted guest at a party and the rest of the class began to look as shocked as David did. They all looked at him, as if expecting him to make the first move...to break the silence.

"I...I..." David tried to speak, but the words seemed to get stuck in his mouth, clinging to his teeth as though even they didn't want to be exposed to this level of awkwardness. Lewis tugged a little on the bottom of David's shirt. That small movement made the whole class jump. Mrs Hawshore's eyes darted from David to the skeleton. Although it was still once again, Mrs Hawshore eyed it with an intensity that seemed as though she was trying to bring it back to life.

David shuddered. The skeleton had always made him feel a little queasy; he never liked looking at it for too long. That tiny shudder was enough to rouse Mrs Hawshore. Her eyes fixed, once again, upon David's and she began to step away from her desk. She was tall for a woman, and had a way of making anybody feel inferior. She got so close him that her nose was almost hanging right over the top of his head. Not knowing where to look, David shut his eyes, trying to rid himself of the feeling of fear which had swept over him. He could feel her breath covering his face, like a toxic gas. He began to back away, his eyes still closed.

What happened next remains, to this day, the scariest thing that David King ever experienced. As he shuffled backwards, making a bid for freedom, something stopped him in his tracks. A bony, grey hand gripped his shoulder so tightly that his body became immobilised. Very slowly, he began to open his eyes, to see what on earth was going on. He had not even got them half way open when he snapped them back shut again, from the shock of what followed.

"YOU MALICIOUS LITTLE BOY! HOW DARE YOU VANDALISE ONE OF MY POSSESSIONS IN SUCH A VIOLENT MANNER! HOW DARE YOU AIM TO DAMAGE ONE OF MY POSSESSIONS AT ALL! DO YOU KNOW HOW HARD I WORKED GATHERING THE BONES OF THAT SKELETON? DO YOU KNOW HOW MANY YEARS WORK I PUT INTO REASSEMBLING IT? I WILL NOT TOLERATE LITTLE BEASTS LIKE YOU THROWING 30 YEARS OF MY HARD WORK DOWN THE DRAIN. YOU IGNORANT LITTLE FOOL!"

A silence hung in the air, so absolute it was as if nobody would ever breathe again. Whether out of sheer fright or by the force of Mrs Hawshore's hand, David crumpled into his chair, a few little tears appearing in the corner of his eye. He couldn't even move to wipe them away. The only person in the whole room that was moving was Mrs Hawshore. She scooted over to her beloved skeleton, examined every bone, tapped it on the shoulder and fled from the room.

The children in the class were utterly shocked and, after remaining still for around ten minutes, began to follow suit and leave the room. Each child's face was as pale as the paper in their notebooks, and the urgency with which they left the room suggested they wanted to stay for not a second longer.

David and Lewis were the last to leave. Regardless of the fact that it wasn't even noon, they grabbed their bags and headed straight through the school gates and out into the village.

Neither one of them spoke for about an hour. The first one to break this streak of silence was Lewis.

"Well, she got you that time mate."

David's lips pursed and his stomach dropped. Lewis was right.

"I...I..."

"Nah, don't worry. I've got it sussed."

"W...what do you mean?" David forgot to be pleased he was finally managing to speak again, because he was so eager to hear what it was Lewis was planning.

"You leave it to me. Put it this way... she won't feel half as fond of that skeleton next time she sees it."

"L...Lewis, what...?"

"Look, if you really want to know meet me tomorrow, early. We've got biology first, correct?"

"Correct."

Lewis turned his back and began to walk away, laughing to himself as he went.

That night dragged for David. The anticipation of what was to come stopped him from getting much sleep and so when Lewis appeared outside the butchers the next morning, David was barely awake enough to realise he'd come from inside the shop. It took a few minutes to twig what Lewis was holding. His arms were clutching a crate of something which was dripping a sticky, red substance from one corner.

"What you got there?" David mumbled, rubbing his eyes. Lewis, grinning, pulled back the cover from the top of the crate, revealing several things which made David heave In the crate sat two eyes, two lungs, a liver, a heart and a jar of real blood. "Right...and what do you plan to do with these?"

But Lewis wouldn't tell. The two boys walked to school in silence, occasionally exchanging mischievous smiles.

Upon arriving at school, people usually go straight to their form room and register before going on to their lessons. Lewis and David however, walked right past their form room and Lewis, leading David, hurried along to their biology room. Once in the room, Lewis shut the door, pulled down the blinds and sat the crate on the desk closest to the skeleton.

"Right. Now is our time to shine." He said, pulling the heart out of the crate and weaving it inside the skeleton, so it shone through the bones like a ruby in the snow. "Come on then, get your hands dirty." Lewis winked and David, although shuddering a little at the prospect, grabbed one of the eye balls and positioned it in an eye socket.

In a matter of minutes the boys had emptied the crate and the skeleton was looking gloriously gory.

"Impressive, huh?" Lewis grinned at David.

David examined the skeleton, now dripping with blood and full of highly aromatic organs. He nodded and returned the grin.

Glancing at their watches, the boys rolled up the blinds, kicked the crate underneath a cupboard and ran out of the room, ready to line up with the rest of their class.

Within a few minutes the rest of the glass had arrived, prepared for an hour of boredom.

When Mrs Hawshore arrived, she greeted the class with a miserable grunt of acknowledgment and opened the door for them to file in. At first there was the usual silence. Then, one by one, the class began to struggle to suppress their laughter.

"For goodness sake children," Mrs Hawshore sighed, shutting the door behind the last pupil and turning to take her place at her desk, "it's time to stop with this silly behaviour and get on with our…AAAAAAARGHHHHH!!!."

A more bloodcurdling scream had never been heard. The noise seemed to echo around the room for several minutes – as did the sound of the children's laughter at the look of pure horror upon Mrs Hawshore's face.

For a moment she froze, shaking and pointing and then, with another ear-piercing scream she fled the room, slamming the door behind her.

Mrs Hawshore never returned to teach that class after that day. Memories of the bloodstains upon the bones of her beloved skeleton were enough to restart her screams.

And as for David and Lewis…well they were subjected to a month of detentions and were kicked off their biology course. But… to this day, the legend about the skeleton in the corner of that classroom is enough to cheer up any child enduring painful hours of boredom in biology.

By Anna Lambert

PRINCE XAVIER AND LAZY JOE

One upon a time
Yesterday morning

The cultivated and respected Prince with the heart of an angel
Lazy Joe

Galloped briskly through the bracing invigorating air on his crisp white horse.
Rode on his mucky bike

To meet his beloved Princess Rosa, after a week of not seeing each other.
To face his head teacher as he arrived at school late.

Rosa greeted him, obviously besotted, with a warm hug and a passionate kiss ensued.
The head teacher gave him a stern look.

The Prince apologised for such a long absence and elaborated that he was on a noble quest.
"Sorry, Mr Mordred, I had a rough morning."

"What noble quest did my fearless, chivalrous warrior attend, to have come back to me with such delay?"
Mr Mordred questioned his answer.

"My dearest Rosa, had I not had to do it, I would have been with you in that time, but I had to fight for peace and to save the Lands of Yonder".
"I was mugged and then missed the bus."

"Oh Xavier, had you not thought of letting me know? I was worried sick. Please, do not ever leave me again, my dear!"

"Joe, I'm sick of your excuses! One more late mark and you get detention for a month."

"My beloved darling, I'll never leave you alone again, lonely in this grand, majestic castle. Never!"
"Sorry Sir, it won't happen again".

The future princess forgave her dearest lover, as she had missed him dearly.
It's been quiet without you. It's a shame you're back."

Rosa and the Prince returned to the kingly castle, to reunite with King and Queen.
Joe sat in his seat, next to his friends.

The royal family talked about Prince Xavier's latest crusade, at the dinner table, with a magnificently prepared, delicious feast.
Joe and his mates talked about his morning troubles at lunch.

At the end of the long-lasting day, Prince Xavier rested his in his marvellous bed in his private chamber and drifted off to an adventurous, fantastic dream.
In the evening, Joe decided to go to bed.

By Katarzyna Zawadska

LOST

Running. How long had I been running? For an age it seemed. Why did I agree to this? I knew it was a bad idea. The light was dimming, making it even harder to see the way in front.   I could hear it behind me. Panting. Chasing. Gaining on me.

Running. Moving. Catching up. Must keep up. Red clouded my vision. Frustration. Rage Pain. Bared my teeth. Warning snarl. He would pay. Pay dearly. For me. For her. For them. For us.

I hated these woods. The trees loomed over like spindly old crones from a fantasy novel, waiting to hex me. No one goes into these woods without a reason. A reason I was experiencing first hand. So what if a pelt was worth a great amount? It wasn't worth it. Not for this. Not for anything.

A snarl ripped through the air behind me like a sonic boom, raising the fine hairs on the back of my neck. It was getting closer. The light was dimming: my time was ending.

Gaining on him. Fear scented the air. Sweet. Invigorating. Energising. Sped up. Spotted him: stumbling, frightened. Pathetic. Feet bashed against ground. Eyes adjusted to darkness. Blood pounding. Senses sharpening. Predatory instinct rising. Heading for the kill.

I spotted a clearing up ahead and sprinted towards it. If I could see the beast in the open, I'd have a decent shot at it. I couldn't go back in there for my earlier 'prize'. The others could risk their necks for it if they wanted it that badly. I could have carried on running, but I was tiring quickly, fatigue setting in. Loading my shot gun, I took aim, and waited.

Stopped just before clearing. Saw the odd thing. Deadly. Dangerous. Fatal. Took mother from pups. Alpha from pack. Mate from me. Walked around edge. Kept quiet. Undetected. Invisible. Prey cowering now. Shaking. Weak.

Perfect.

I heard it before I saw it. The twigs cracking under its feet. It slunk around in the shadows, waiting for the opportune moment, sizing me up. Thinking of its chances. It was a fluke I hit the other one. But I couldn't tell it that, could I? I held my breath, awaiting my demise. I was a horrid person, I knew that now. Poaching wasn't a way of life as my brothers had always said. It was a crime, a stupid crime that got people killed. People like me. Suddenly, it pounced. The last thing I saw was a shadow racing towards me: a pitch black shadow with gleaming white teeth and luminous green eyes.

"I'm sorry," I said to it.

The final words I spoke; the ones I'd wanted to say all my life.

Satisfaction. Joy. Relief. Threat gone. Pups safe. Pack safe. Protected. Left creature for others. They would come. Turned to go home. To pups. To pack. To family. Family without her. Family without mate. My mate. Pain strong. Powerful. Overbearing. Bitter. But hope. Still had pack, still had pups, still had title. Still top dog.

By Frances Younger

NO ESCAPE

Along the street ran a scrawny light haired boy. He wasn't much of a man; he wore unstylish clothes and had thin, little arms. He ran on the narrow pavements, dodging cars and lamp posts, with a look of fear in his eyes. He took a sharp turn into an alleyway and sat there, shaking and afraid.

Down the same street hurtled a taller and bigger man. He had dark, ruffled hair and very large muscles. He took the same route only running down the centre of the road. He kept looking left and then right, and then left and then right. He had signs of aggression on his face. He asked pedestrians about where the young boy had gone and when someone told him the answer he wanted to hear, he simply smiled. He turned slowly and stood, towering over him and just as he was about to grab him, the boy escaped and this time he sprinted at a much faster rate.

The young man was now quaking with terror as he dashed down the dark alleyway, causing a mess behind him. The young boy was sweating as his options of escape were becoming limited. As he came to the end of the alleyway, he saw a small hole in a mesh fence, just big enough for him to fit through. But not for the guy chasing him.

As the larger man jumped over bins and obstacles left behind from the boy, he came to the end of the alleyway. Only to find himself all alone. He would have turned around and given up, had he not heard the rustling of dry leaves coming from the small woodland situated behind a mesh fence.

After making his way through the hole, catching his top on the sharp wires and in turn cutting his shoulder, the boy carefully positioned himself out of sight from the man. He was behind large oak tree and he waited until the man's shadow was visible and then he sat there, quiet as a mouse, breathing lightly and holding his breath. Unfortunately, even though he moved only slightly, he made a large noise in the leaves. When he saw the man climbing over the fence towards him, he ran for his life. Always looking over his shoulder. But suddenly he lost his footing and the ground beneath him vanished. He then found himself hurtling down a hill, landing on his back in the leaves, with a surging pain in his legs. He then, just lay there waiting for his chaser to finally catch up with him.

As the man came to him, panting for breath, he stared at the young boy, and shouted viciously at him, with a voice full of rage. He picked up the young boy up by his collar and then he threw the young offender into his police car.

By Sophie Cancemi

I GUESS I SHOULD HAVE LISTENED

I guess I should have listened. Things might be different right now. I might not be standing here alone. Wishing for something that can never be mine. My sister was right. I shouldn't have trusted Him. Now...now I'm all alone. My sister took my fall. She paid the price that I should have paid. She was punished instead off me.

I guess I should have listened. Deep down I suppose I knew something about him was wrong. Knew there was some deadly secret. But I loved him too much to care. I was bitten by the love bug. And now I have nothing no sister, no love. Because He stole it all. He drew me in and trapped me in a web of lies and deceit like a spider cocoons a fly before sucking it dry. My sister warned me. She said he was using me to get close to Dad. Our Dad, the famous rock singer who cared more about his guitar than his daughters.

I guess I should have listened. Dad hardly ever noticed us. I bet he will notice now. What I've done and what I'm about to do will stay in his mind forever. And I hope he feels guilty about not noticing. I hope he regrets his obsession with his fans, his guitar, and his shows. They pushed me and my sister out. He pushed us out. So now I'm going. My sister has been taken but I've got to go now. I've got to let them take me too.

I guess I should have listened. I see the event clearly. Him pulling out the knife, with a mad, Machiavellian look in his red, blood-flecked eyes. Him telling me to move aside. That he needed to cause my Dad the same pain he'd caused Him. I hear me refusing and yelling at him to go away. I hear the front door open and my sister come out. I see her asking what's going on. Him replying and her ordering him to leave. I see him refusing. He charges at my sister, his pewter black hair blowing back. She doesn't move. Determined to protect our Dad, even though he wouldn't protect her. I hear her gasp and see her icy blue eyes widen as the knife slides into her stomach. I see the blood flow.

He just laughs, a manic glint in his eye as he pulls the knife out. My sister falls to the ground and lies motionless. I feel an animal roar of pain, rage, fear and grief rip from my throat as she collapses. I punch him in the face. I want to make him hurt. I rip the knife from his grasp and stab him over and over and over in a blood-rage. I can no longer hear anything but the blood pounding in my head as I throw his lifeless body to the ground and run to my sister. I call her name. Urge her to open her eyes. But she does not. I check for a pulse desperate for there to be one. But I know there won't be and there isn't. I sob, tears carving tracks in the blood on my cheeks and dripping into my sisters blood stained, brunette hair.

I guess I should have listened. I don't know how long I sat there with my sister. I was numb. But eventually I moved. I stole my Dad's car and drove to her beach. To my sister's special beach. The one she and I found together. I gently lift my sister's body and walk into the surf. I place her carefully in the current that I know never reaches land again. She told me. My sister researched it and found that out. She was smart. Now the tears on my cheeks are for us both. For her lost life and for mine. I watch the current drag her away from me. I whisper "Goodbye".

I guess I should have listened. And now stand here alone. Friendless and without a family. I sigh. And look up at the clouds I know my sister will be seated amongst the angels. Feasting on the best of everything. She is at peace now I know. I may or may not join her up there, but I know that I will never forget her or forgive him.

I guess I should have listened. With a sad smile I walk into deeper waters. The stones I attached to my feet preventing me from floating, the never ending current pulling me in. The water reaches my chest, my neck, my chin. It covers my mouth as I carry on walking. Soon the waves are up to my sea green eyes. I hear a shout behind me. Maybe my Dad or some innocent passer-by. But I don't care. I don't look back I just carry on walking.

I guess I should have listened. As the water covers my head my beach blonde hair floats out behind me. I breathe in and the water rushes up my nose. I don't surface. I just keep going. I see the sea shelf, where the sea bed drops suddenly, and I pull myself out the never-ending current. I walk towards it, the downwards current speeding my progress. I step over the edge and sink into the dark, gloomy depths of the ocean dragged by the stones and the sea. Towards the ravine bed. Towards my final resting place. Towards my final bed. My bed where I will lay down for my sleep. Where the spiders can't reach me or suck me dry.

By Lauren Miller

FINDING THE PHOENIX

I picked up the book; felt it's smooth leather cover. Out of all the books in the shop it had caught my eye as soon as I walked in there. "Mum I'm just buying this book, I'll be two minutes".

"Okay, hurry up though; I need to get to my spinning class for four."

I paid for the book and quickly raced out the shop so I could catch up with mum. I couldn't wait to get home so I could start reading it. Mum was waiting for me just outside the shop. I showed her the book, she wasn't interested at all.

After we had some lunch mum left me outside the coffee shop and went off to her spinning class, I wanted to get home quickly so I called Marcus and got him to pick me up.

"Hey little bro, what you been up to?" After getting in the car Marcus soon tried to start making conversation. I wasn't in the mood for talking to Marcus. I've never really liked Marcus, he's my half-brother and he's always picking on me and mum doesn't bat an eyelid when he's flicking me and nicking my trainers. So I didn't answer him and stayed silent the whole car drive home.

As soon as I got home I ran upstairs into my bedroom, closed the door, and jumped on my bed. I got out the book and started flicking through it. I stopped at one page that caught my eye and stopped to read it thoroughly. 'Near the end of the Phoenix's life it builds itself a nest of twigs. The Phoenix then sets itself alight in the nest so both the nest and it are reduced to ashes. From the ashes, a Phoenix egg emerges which soon hatches and a young Phoenix is born.' I turned to the next page and a piece of paper fell out of the book and into my lap. I looked down to see a drawing of a cave. I then remembered back to a photo mum had shown me of her and dad which was taken a year before dad died. On the photo they were stood at the bottom of a cliff. Halfway up the cliff there was a cave which looked identical to the one in the drawing.

Later that day I asked mum about the photo of her and dad. She told me that the place where it was taken was only 15 miles away from where we lived. I decided that I would ride my bike up to the cliff and investigate the cave because if the drawing was in a book about the mythical, magical, magnificent creature called a Phoenix then the cave must be connected to the book.

A week later I was ready and I got my bike out of the shed, pumped up the wheels and cycled all the way to the cave as fast as I could (I got a little lost on the way but I got there eventually). When I got there I used the stuff from dad's rock climbing bag that I borrowed and made my way up the cliff to the cave. It was hard but I managed to get up to the cave. If mum had known what I was doing she would have freaked, but I told her I was going for a bike ride to my mates' house.

I entered the cave. It was really dark inside so I got a torch from my bag and I looked around; there wasn't much there and it was quite small but I noticed something at the back of the cave in the corner. There was a rather large egg. I remembered the book and I took it out of my bag I frantically flicked through till I found the right page. '...from the ashes a Phoenix egg emerges which soon hatches and a young Phoenix is born'. I couldn't believe it.

If I was right, then that egg was a Phoenix egg and in less than a week it would hatch and a new Phoenix would be born. I came back every day for the next 5 days checking the egg, sitting next to it and talking to it. Until Saturday morning I woke up and I knew that was the day it should hatch. It said in the book, 'the egg hatches in 6 days'. I arrived at the cave early and I quietly walked to the back of the cave to find nothing...

I looked everywhere in the tiny cave but there was no young Phoenix and no egg. I ran outside into the morning sun and sat down on a rock. "I was so stupid to think that was a Phoenix egg, it was probably just a large bird or something," I said sadly to myself but then I saw it. It flew right past me, its beautiful wings soaring through the sky. I stood up and it flew to me, then stood next to me on the cliff and looked at me. I think it liked me because I sat and talked to it while it was still inside the egg.

To this day I still feel like I'm living a dream, because every time I go visit the Phoenix it just seems so unreal but no one has seen my Phoenix and no one will. I found the Phoenix.

By Darcy Shaw

Group Four

Secondary School Poetry

A MORE THAN ANXIOUS WAIT

He stood there silently,
Staring at the door.
A panic prevented bead of sweat
Fell to the floor.
His big clammy hand
Pulled the door that said push,
In moments like this
His sense turned to mush.

His heart was a bird,
Trapped in a cage of ribs,
Flying around madly,
He had a pulse in his jib.
BOOM BOOM went his heart,
In out went his breath,
He felt like he was dying,
He felt he was near death.

She demanded his name,
He told her in despair.
She ordered him to sit,
And he collapsed in a chair.

He ran a shaky hand
Through his gelled black thorns.
And he wished at that moment,
That he'd never been born.
He dashed to the toilet,
Emptied his disturbed bowel.
He sniffed his sweaty underarms,
Boy he smelt foul!

He splashed his perspiring face,
Once twice and again.
Slapped his pale cheeks,
And prepared to face the lion's den.
His hands were moist with sweat,
They slipped and missed the door handle.
Those on the other side laughed.
His face flushed hot like a candle.

He sat there uncomfortably.
Wringing his hands.
A ridiculous specimen,
Of a forty year old man.
He tapped his foot nervously,
Just couldn't keep still.
Those next to him glared at him,
With looks that could kill.
He felt 100 degrees
His heartbeat in his ears.
This was the worst,
Worst of all his fears.
Then the time came,
The event for which he had waited.
His bottom lip trembled,
His pupils dilated.

He slowly rose from his chair,

His body quivering at all
angles.
Yet he knew that this was
something,
That he could not wangle.
He opened the giant door,
Let it slam behind.
And for a moment was
completely numb,
A blank moment in his mind.

He began to walk that
daunting walk,
Feeling like a man on Death
Row.
Sweat gathered on his
forehead,
He couldn't feel his toes.
But he kept on going, going,
Although he thought the room
appeared to be shrinking.
He bounced off a wall, tripped
on his lace,
Just didn't know what he was
thinking.

At last he saw her smiling at
him,
His idea of the Devil.
He felt all faint, all weak and
limp,
He felt in mortal peril.
His body quaked like a
shivering dog,
As he lowered himself in the
chair.

He closed his eyes-tight as he
could,
As he faced this atrocious
nightmare.

Ping ping went her gloves,
Ring ring went her phone.
He felt so isolated,
Utterly and completely alone.
"Open up" she demanded,
His mouth was locked tight.
He had to prize it open,
Using all his willpower and
might.

She tapped and poked his
teeth,
With her evil weapons.
And he could feel somewhere,
deep inside his soul,
What was about to happen.
She lightly poked his back
molars,
With her wedding finger.
He knew the time was here,
He could no longer linger.

With a great and almighty
crunch,
He bit her finger clean off.
She screamed like a hellish
banshee,
As her finger he chewed and
scoffed.
Her blood squirted all over,
The floor and windows and
walls.

And he felt something inside
of him,
Something not right at all.

He obviously felt pretty awful,
He couldn't help his reaction
to the dentist.
But he felt a pain inside of him,
As though he'd been punched
by a fist.
Suddenly it came to him,
The dentist's wedding ring!
His face began to swell,
And his eyes began to sting.

He clasped his throat and fell
to the ground,
Or so I'm told,
And all this happened due to
the fact
He had an allergy to gold!
He lay there next to the
dentist,
Who had collapsed at the sight
of blood,

The dental nurse ran about
screaming,
Doing everything she could.

That night when discharged
from the hospital,
After having the ring pulled
out,
He came home and told his
wife,
Who gave him such a clout.
She told him he was ridiculous,
Grown men aren't scared of
the dentist!
He went bright red, got quite
mad
And ended up having quite a
tiz!

She told him one important
thing,
She called it her 'golden rule',
"Never go back to the dentist,"
she said,
"You finger gobbling fool!"

By Clara Dunphy

THE NORTHERN LIGHTS

As the night comes along,

And down goes the sun,

Merry stars begin to shine.

In great jubilation,

And exhilaration.

The Aurora reigns on high.

A twisting spectrum of noble hues,

With golden, greens, reds and blues,

A battle of phantoms, magic abounding,

The time is nigh,

The Aurora is sounding.

Restrained by no tether,

Abrading of the ether,

Magnetic crusaders combine.

In leaps and bounds,

A rip roar of sounds,

A foxtrot to the beat of time.

Weaving the twine of existence,

Mocking the mortal viewer.

Expressing control and persistence.

Blazing ever truer

By George Pickering

REFLECTIONS

She's watching me.
She's watching me cry.
No sympathy in her eyes.
She stares cold, hard, deep
into me.
Confusion as to why she
shows no emotion
screams through my mind.
Something's not right.
Something's very wrong.
How can she smile while
watching me cry?
She's not even trying to
help.
She's frozen in her stare.
Eyes locked on mine.
My tears blur her out for a
second,
and when I look back,
she's changed.
Her staring smile,
forced to tears.
She's breaking down in front
of me.
I don't understand this.
She looks so lost.
Not at all familiar.
But wait,
I can feel her tears.
Why do I feel her tears that
fall?
She looks down,
as her perfect marble tears
roll away from her cheek.
I stare back.
How can this be?
She was smiling at me.
Staring at me.
Was she staring at me?
Or behind me?
Maybe through me?
It makes no sense.
My tears have stopped,
yet I'm frozen in place.
My eyes now trapped in her
every marble tear drop.
As they hit the ground,
I feel my stare move from
tear to eye.
I'm looking at her.
Not behind her.
Not even through her.
I'm just... staring.
It feels familiar,
like I've done this before.
But her face is so cold and
hard to recognise.
Why do I feel her tears fall?
She whimpers,
and a cord strikes.
Her voice.
How could this be?
It's not possible.
Her pain wrenches through
me.
My heart stops.

I reach to stop my own pain.
My hand is moving for her.
But I don't understand.
I'm in pain yet I reach for
her.
She's reaching back.
What's happening?
I'm feeling so lost.
I touch her heart, and she
touches mine.
Our eyes lock in a dazed
stare.
We've frozen in our fears,
pains, stares.
Can it be,
that she is me,
and I, am she?

By Bethany Davies

GAMES, GAMES, GAMES

Games, Games, Games,
There are so many from which to choose,
How do I know which to play?
Will I win or lose?

I didn't win at tennis,
I didn't win at squash,
I didn't win at badminton,
I guess that means I lost!

I thought I'd try computer games,
I started with the PS3,
Next I tried the Xbox,
Now I'm on the Wii!

Chess was far too difficult,
Draughts was just too boring,
Snakes and ladders took too long,
Now everyone is snoring!

How about a team game,
Footballs the one for me,
I've made it to the Olympics,
Go team GB!

Games, Games, Games,

There are still so many to choose,

And in the end it doesn't matter,

Whether I win or lose!

By Amber Kingsland

TIME

How do you run from something that's already got you?
Trapped in a net of a monster produced in the most twisted part
of hell,
A pin sunk deep into my bubble of hope.
Waiting is all I have left.

What can you do when your good isn't good enough?
When each mole hill becomes a mountain?
When the colours begin to fade to black?
Waiting is all I have left.

How do you suck out the poison if a hole was never there?
I wait for the last grain of sand to fall in the hour glass;
The dagger hovering above my head.
Waiting is all I have left.

How do I take my mind off the chilled muzzle of the gun that
borrows deep into my temple?
A twisted finger latched surely on the trigger.
Waiting is all I have left.

Seconds like hours, the trigger pulls,
I stop running from what has me,
I stop climbing over mountains,
The colours finally fade to black,
The poison satisfies its hunger,
The last grain of sand has fallen,
The dagger has dropped,
Waiting is all I have left.

By Hollie Plester

SUNRISE AND SUNSET

The morning sun, so bright and cheerful,
Would make the winter even more cold and fearful.
I lay down staring into the clouds,
Making in my mind butterflies and clowns.
The mountains in the distance look like pointy rocks,
but when you're up close you can't see their tops.
As the day draws in I get sleepy,
and the scene around me feels so dreamy.
The sunset sky hovers over the tropical sea,
I watch as the golden globe above stares down at me.
As it starts to disappear just above the sealine,
the beautiful sunset colour starts to decline.
The water starts to lose its glistening shimmer,
and the sky above gets dimmer and dimmer.
The tropical sky has now gone,
and the tropical moonlit night has begun.
I watch as the moon steals the sun's light,
and shines amongst the dark sky so bright.
The stars look like fireflies all around,
Millions of them shining there mini lights onto the ground.
The white pearl in the pitch black sky,
gradually moves away with the stars up high.
And as they go, the tropical sky comes back to say hello,
and the day starts again with a sky crimson yellow.

By Romanie-Jade Tulloch

Prayer, Positive Thin
Mom's S

INTRODUCTION

This story is a recap of the past eight months. I wrote it as a way to try to remember and appreciate just what has happened and how very far we have come.

Mom has little or no recollection of the trauma she has been through. She doesn't really remember any of the hospitalizations or the chemotherapy. She has no memory of the side effects of the radiation or the struggles we have gone through to save her life.

So, in some small way, perhaps she can read her story and realize that she is indeed a medical phenomenon.

What we have accomplished through prayer, positive thinking and protein is nothing short of a miracle.

I'd like to introduce you to my mom, Delores Mikula. She comes from a long line of strong women. Her mother lived to be 100 years old and her older sister is soon to be 92.

Before mom became ill she was nursing her older sister back to health for the third time. The first time was due to the dreaded cancer which required chemotherapy treatment. She spent the fall and winter months under moms care and resumed living at home for several years where she was also a caregiver to her ailing husband. The second time she lived with mom was after a car accident that put her in the hospital with a fractured hip. After the hip replacement she spent her required number of days in a rehab facility and the winter with mom. The last time she was moms patient she was discovered on the floor with her cell phone in her hand, incoherent and reciting the Lord's prayer non-stop for 48 hours. After being hospitalized for a few weeks and a month or so in a nursing home we busted her out and she has been recovering nicely with my mom's Tender Loving Care.

Mom has been the quintessential caregiver to her family for many years. She cared for dad, who had black lung, for over fifteen years of illness. She kept grandma at home with her for over a year. Both dad and grandma passed away in her house.

Mom does not believe in nursing homes. You take care of your own at home. "None of my loved ones will ever be put in a nursing home." She kept her word on that.

I can't tell you how old mom is because I'm not allowed. People ask me all the time" how old is your mother?" and I say "she won't tell me" Of course I know but I keep her secret.

Mom has been the second mother to her grandchildren and even the primary parent to her oldest great grandchild who she raised for nine years. At the age of 74 she was once again a kindergarten mother. She baked cupcakes, attended PTA meetings and parent teacher conferences.

She was a youthful 84 years old when she became stricken with cancer. It manifested itself in a most horrific way by actually breaking her neck. This neck pain was ignored until it became so painful that it rendered her helpless. I'm guessing that her tolerance to pain must be extraordinary.

She never complained about anything except for high prices or bad weather. Never said she was sick or even tired.

She was active in church functions and was installed a few years ago as a deacon. She was always available to serve at church dinners and help out with bible school and with special programs for the children.

I never heard the word no come out of my mother's mouth. She would do anything for her children or grandchildren. She loved us all unconditionally.

She is very special to us and I have often said I want to be just like her when I grow up.

If ever you were in need she would be the first to lend a hand.

She always showed more concern for others than for herself. I think this is the secret to a long happy life.

I remember my grandmother saying that she was having leg cramps and she said "I could hardly get up out of the chair to answer the door and get the neighbor boy a cookie" "I think he could have missed his daily cookie for one day don't you think gram" "oh no, he was expecting his cookie I didn't want to disappoint him." I really think this is how she lived to be 100. She was unconcerned about her own pain. She wanted to be good to others.

This is exactly how my mother is. Good to others.

 It all began on Thanksgiving Day 2011 Mom had cooked dinner as usual for the crowd. During dinner she began to cry in pain. Her neck was hurting to the extent that she couldn't bear it. I had never seen my mother cry. Perhaps she shed a tear, maybe, at funerals or weddings.

Had I known what lie ahead she would have been immediately taken to the hospital. Who would have ever suspected the horror that we were about to endure.

The following Monday a chiropractic appointment was made and she seemed to be feeling somewhat better. Over the weekend I recall offering her both heat and ice, whichever one felt better to make her neck stop hurting. Once again, hindsight being 20/20 it never occurred to any of us that this stiff neck could be a serious problem.

On Sunday the 11ᵗʰ of December Women's Fellowship of Bethel Church held its monthly meeting in the church basement. We had dinner and assembled baby kits for the "Center of Hope" (a nonprofit organization chosen to support). We addressed Christmas cards for the shut-ins in the nursing homes. The neck became much worse. Wrongly I attributed this to being bent over the table for long periods of time addressing cards and wrapping gifts and the overall overwork involved with the season.

Monday morning another chiropractic appointment was made. I was halfway down the mountain when my cell phone rang. It was mom asking if I could take her to the appointment. She said "I hate to bother you at work but you know I wouldn't ask if I really didn't need help." This should have thrown another red flag up because mom never asked for help, especially on a work day. I turned around at the bottom of the mountain and went to her house where I found she was not even able to dress herself. Dr. Will Moffott did a very gentle adjustment and scheduled her for another appointment for the next morning.

Tuesday was the office Christmas party that I had planned for the girls at my office. I'm fortunate enough to be the practice manager for our small town physician's office. My office is the location of my mom's primary care physician. We were soon to find out that this will certainly come in handy as the days and months progress.

Mom had a follow-up appointment with the chiropractor that morning. After some x-rays and a recommendation to get a CT-scan later we were headed out of the chiropractic office when mom began to throw up due to the pain. I called our office and Brenda scheduled her for the scan the next morning.

Later that day, I was enjoying the luncheon and the tour when my husband, Sonny, called and told me I needed to get back over to mom's house. Not wanting to leave mom alone, he had volunteered to hang around and trim some branches in the driveway in case she needed anything. I arrived to find mom in excruciating pain unable to even scoot herself up in bed. We couldn't even move her without her screaming. Sonny and I convinced mom that she needed to go to the hospital by ambulance. She agreed but only if I would ride in the ambulance with her. They wouldn't let me ride in the back so I rode up front. I immediately called my sister Mary and told her to meet us at the hospital.

The ER doctor ordered some x-rays and a CT-Scan. The waiting seemed forever. He returned and said he would like to transfer mom to Presbyterian Hospital in Pittsburgh under the pretense that the hospital was completely full and that they had no available beds. Not knowing the real reason, we protested and wanted her to stay right in the ER bed until one became available. Ruby Memorial was a full hour closer. Why not Ruby? "They won't answer the phone" said the ER Doctor. "Seriously" we said.

After much debate back and forth with Mary and me the ER doctor finally admitted that the reason she needed to be transferred was that her CT-scan had revealed that she had a tumor of unknown origin in her neck which was causing her the intense pain. She will need to be evaluated and the tumor will need biopsied immediately. Presby was the hospital that he felt was the best choice. We sort of felt that this is because UPMC partners with the Uniontown Hospital. I doubt very much that Ruby Memorial simply did not answer the phone.

The ER doctor insisted that she go to Presby so the ambulance was called and again I found myself in the front of the ambulance with Mom in the back. Sonny followed to bring me home. All the while thinking that this will be a minor event and the mass will be extracted from her neck and all will be done and over in just a matter of a day or two. *WRONG!!!*

CHAPTER TWO
The Shock

Upon arrival at the hospital and going through afterhours security I met up with the gurney and followed mom and the medics to a holding room. It was great she had a nurse who had only one other empty bed in this completely private block of enclosed rooms. The nurse called in a neurosurgeon, which ordered the necessary tests and admitted her. This was the last time I saw this particular neurosurgeon.

I soon found out that nothing happens quickly in a hospital.

Still under the delusion that this was only going to be a few days in the hospital then home again. We had plenty of time left to finish Christmas shopping and get everything ready. I had made a to-do list. I was ready. As I read it off to Sonny in the car on the way to the hospital the next day. He said "yeah right." Rule number one don't ever think you can be ahead of schedule.

The next day turned into the next evening and without any news or plan as of yet in place we were getting quite antsy. The nurses were phenomenal, they called the doctors in charge and they finally sent one down to mom's room to speak to us.

By this time mom was wearing a very uncomfortable, rigid, oversized neck collar that made it all but impossible for her to move not only her head but her entire body. A person really doesn't realize how much you rely on your neck when you move.

Rule of thumb: if a doctor makes no eye contact and starts out each sentence with "*I'm sorry, but*" you can count on one thing....... whatever this person says you are not going to like it, accept it, or believe it.

We didn't even try to remember all the names of all the doctors who came in and out to offer up their opinions. We found it easier to think of someone that they looked like and actually renamed all of them. The first one we spoke with, and the one that really made an impact on us, was a taller version of our cousin's son Matthew. So, this intern became known to us as "Tall Matthew". Tall Matthew made no eye contact and started each sentence with "I'm sorry, but". He gave us his diagnosis and plan of treatment and you guessed it we didn't like it, accept it or believed it.

He began by saying that mom's life as she knows it will never be the same. Her reserve will be greatly impacted by the treatments she will need to undergo. Each time an elderly person has a procedure done they deplete there reserve.

First off no one calls our mother elderly. She certainly is not, nor never has been elderly. He recommends that she be treated with radiation to reduce the tumor. She will continue wearing the cumbersome collar. Upon recovery from the radiation, which could take as much as a year, perhaps, surgery to repair the damage to the neck? He felt that the tumor would not be

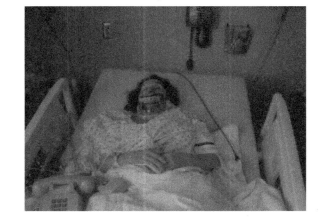

easily removed and that this would be the least invasive course of action.

Doctor number two who will be called "Clark Kent" because of his striking resemblance to the cartoon version of Superman, had a different course of action. "We may certainly be able to completely remove this tumor surgically and repair the neck and do the biopsy all at the same time."

Our hero! Yes! This is the doctor we will like, accept and believe.

We also found out that in a hospital nothing ever happens when you are in the room waiting. Simply step out of the room go to the bathroom or go to the cafeteria and everything will happen while you are gone. They plan it that way…they have spy's.

You find yourself waiting for simply hours on everything from test results to Kleenex. Ask and you shall sometime today or maybe tomorrow receive.

The final answer was that a biopsy will be done on Friday morning and the next step determined by the result of the test. Still all the while thinking that this mass or tumor is

just a random fatty type lymph node that will be removed and nothing more will need to be done. Mom will be home for Christmas pain free and ready to enjoy the holidays.
WRONG!!

CHAPTER THREE
Worst Case Scenario

We arrived at the hospital very early the morning of the biopsy at mom's request. We truly believed that the doctor would find an operable tumor which he would remove and mom's pain and suffering would be over and she would be home recovering in just a matter of days.

Mom didn't want to be seen without her teeth so her chief complaint to us when we arrived was "why did they take my teeth so soon?" Being the dutiful daughter that I am I offered to keep the teeth with me so that there was no room for error and that she could resume wearing them as soon as she opened her eyes. I really didn't mind having the teeth with me but they actually chattered every time I made a move. I wanted them to be back in her mouth so badly but unfortunately that was not the case. Those dentures were to ride around chattering in my purse for nearly a week. This would be the first of several conversations I had with the traveling teeth.

We were really blindsided by the next series of events. "Superman" or "Clark Kent" told us that he would be doing the biopsy through the nose. This would be less invasive than actually opening up her neck. The recovery time would be shorter and the anesthesia would be less harmful overall. He said if the only thing they are able to complete is the biopsy the procedure should take about 45 minutes to an hour. If they are able to completely resect the tumor they will be in surgery for approximately two or three hours. After the first hour passed we thought ….yes…..they are able to take the complete tumor. **WRONG!!!**

We finally hear them call "the Mikula family". We stormed the desk. "The doctor will meet with you in the linen closet". At least that's how big it was. We entered in one door and "superman" entered in the other side. He made no eye contact and started his sentence with "I'm sorry, but" Oh boy, we are not going to like this, accept this or believe this. He continued by saying " We were unable to remove the tumor but we have sent out a biopsy. Based on previous experience this tumor is more likely than not a form of myeloma which is a form of cancer." "we have sent the sample to pathology for confirmation" "during the procedure, which we performed nasally, your mother had a stroke and it became necessary to intubate her which we were trying to avoid, she will be on a ventilator until such time that she will be able to breathe on her own" "we won't know until she becomes conscious whether there are any long term debilities from the stroke" "she could experience paralysis of some form, speech or hearing impairment ". The portion to the brain affected controls the sense of balance, coordination and *breathing*" "any questions?" Breathing!!!!!!!!!! We all just stopped.

CHAPTER FOUR
The Vigil

The next several days were spent holding vigil at the bedside. We simply didn't know exactly what was going to happen next we went from an upbeat good day to a 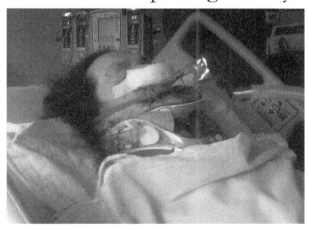 devastating bad day. This turned out to be the pattern that we have come to expect even today.

On our way to the room to see mom for the first time we met up with the anesthesiologists who had been in the operating room. They made no eye contact and started their sentence with "I'm sorry, but".

After the hugs and the apologies we found mom in a monitored ICU with tubes and equipment from every limb. We were quiet, scared and mostly in shock.

Mom was treated by cardiologists with blood thinners. The blood thinners caused her nose to bleed quite heavily. Ear Nose and Throat specialists were called in to treat the nosebleeds.   Her nasal passages were packed with what looked quite a bit like mini tampons with strings hanging down and all.

We spent the following weeks spending two hours in the car, followed by twelve to fourteen hours balancing in hospital window sills or taking turns on the one chair, followed by two more hours in the car, followed by four hours of sleep......lather, rinse, repeat.

The waiting room was inhabited by a very large family that we found out later had been holding vigil for over a month.   They had blankets, pillows, small children crawling on the floor who required strollers and diaper bags. They conducted phone conversations to banks and government agencies as we looked on in embarrassment that we were overhearing this. After they ordered six dozen, garlic hot wings to be delivered it became clear that we needed to find another spot.   Not to mention we really felt we did not belong when the one lady yelled out to the nurse "Hey, we need more towels in our bathroom".

Of course on the next to the last day in the ER we finally found, just one floor below, a very nice quiet waiting room without any overnight occupants.

Mom was showing signs of progress with each passing day.   I will never forget how wonderful it felt seeing her open her eyes, smile and speak for the first time. Multiple times a day either a doctor or a nurse would come in and ask "What is your name?..... And your date of birth?" "Squeeze my fingers, push me away, pull me toward you. Step on the gas, pull up your toes" Excellent!!   Wish I had a nickel for the number of times we heard that routine.

Throughout this entire ordeal Mom continued to be her pleasant, wonderfully sweet self.   I seriously did not know how she could be so adorable, in light of feeling, what

I would consider, the equivalent of being struck by a bus. Nurses fell in love with her. Not a single complaint.

After about two days of vigilance they attempted to remove the ventilator tube. The moment of truth. Can she breathe on her own? Unfortunately, the blood thinner caused the throat to fill with blood and they were fearful that she would choke. They would need to use a camera to remove this so the first attempt failed. It was another day until they tried again. What I didn't realize was that during the day they had already tested her without the ventilator being on…..they knew she could breathe on her own. News I really would have liked to know.

They called in the ENT chief of staff to remove the tampon packing's from her nose. My guess is the interns wanted no part of this responsibility. He was a tall big framed older guy (by older, I mean almost my age.) clearly not his first rodeo. He swooped in made a few cocky references to his Harley Davidson and in just a brief minute or two had removed the tampons.

With the bleeding under control they were again considering making an attempt to remove the breathing tube. This time it was a success. Mom could now speak much clearer only with a very hoarse voice and I reluctantly asked the nurse if she could take over the possession of the chattering, traveling teeth.

CHAPTER FIVE

The Duration

We were closing in on Christmas and hoping for a discharge to home but the closest thing we could receive as our Christmas gift was a step down to a private room.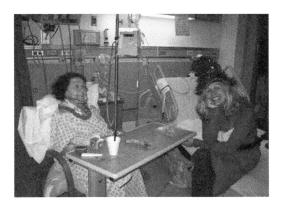

Christmas Eve and Christmas Day were spent at the hospital. Gifts remain un-exchanged to this day. All we wanted was our mom back home.

Because of the stroke the doctors in charge decided that Mom would need a few weeks of physical therapy at a rehab facility. So, Tuesday after Christmas she was loaded up in an ambulance and headed for Healthsouth in Morgantown, WVA.

The room was very nice with a view of the patio. The trees were wrapped in white lights maybe not just for the holidays but for atmosphere.

Mary and I set out to make a few allies. It always helps to find at least one nurse you can complement with the ulterior motive of a little co-operation.

It seemed like every few minutes we were telling someone else the story. "Gee, what happened to you? Did you fall down? Then we had to give the entire synopsis. We always found it important to stress that only a few short weeks ago she was totally independent and working her butt off getting ready for the holidays. This somehow, we hoped, made them realize we hadn't been neglecting her and that she only recently became this ill.

No one really knew how stable her neck was at this point so we were on pins and needles. We were afraid that one wrong move and they could paralyze her or worse. Leaving her alone with them was out of the question. So.....once again we spent an hour in the car followed by many hours in the rehab facility followed by another hour in the car followed by a quick nap…….Lather, rinse, repeat.

Still……mom remained pleasant, cooperative and sweet with everyone. How does she do it? I'm impressed now don't you think I'm not. In the same circumstance I would not be this adorable. What a terrific role model she is for her entire family. We can't let her down…..we just can't.

Christmas was spent in Presby and now New Years at Healthsouth. Little did we know that Valentine's Day and St. Patrick's Day would be spent in Ruby Memorial.

After about the third week of inactivity, coupled with the tremendous amounts of blood thinners and steroids, we began to notice a slight skin tear on her behind. This would later come back to bite us in the butt. Her inability to roll over due to the unstable neck caused pressure on the bum. This should never have happened because until they realized that she could and should get up and walk around the damage was done.

We were three weeks into this hospitalization and the original crisis had not been address yet. What to do with the cancer? We were no farther ahead than we were three weeks ago when we first set foot in the emergency room. If anything we were in deeper trouble because now there had been a stroke which complicated the neck situation even further.

I began to check into oncology appointments. We scheduled one for the 5th of January at Mary Babb Randolph Cancer Center. This was only a short block away and hopefully she could be transported there and back by wheel chair van. Medical records had to be transferred and pathology reports needed to be made available. This is where it pays off to be in the healthcare field. The average person would not be able to say just fax those records to me. But…..if you work for the patient's primary care physician you can easily get what you need.

Her follow-up visit was scheduled for the discharge day from Healthsouth. We had mom in a private vehicle for the first time since mid December. Her oncologist had referred her to an orthopedic surgeon for an evaluation. Dr John France immediately ordered an x-ray and instantly decided that her neck was not stable enough to go home. She was direct admitted and scheduled for surgery ASAP. Unfortunately the blood thinners had to be stopped for three days prior to surgery. So on Friday the thirteenth I took possession once again of the chattering, traveling teeth.

CHAPTER SIX
The Surgery

It was Friday the thirteenth of January. Mom was prepped for surgery we were meeting with the anesthesiologist at her bedside in the surgical holding area. This particular doctor seemed very confident and assured us that she would be in the very best of hands. They would be trying to keep her sedated without intubation if possible. This was particularly scary knowing that her life hung in the balance. One wrong move and she could be paralyzed or worse. The spinal column was impinged upon by the tumor. The broken vertebras were to be replaced with cadaver bones, rods pins and screws.

Once again we found ourselves in the waiting room. This wait seemed particularly long though the entire procedure took just over five hours. We were the last family standing…….. Or should I say sitting. We spotted Dr. France in an adjacent waiting area speaking with another family. This is good if something went wrong he would have surely spoken with us first......or it went wrong and he wishes to speak with us alone in case we freak out. Finally after what seemed like a very long time he came over to our cubicle, sat down, crossed his legs, made eye contact (this was huge) and proceeded to tell us that the surgery went well. "They try to make the neck as normal looking as possible so they put it all in place temporarily and then they all step back and take a look. Once everyone is satisfied they rivet it." He said it was similar to puttying a car. "You want it to appear as normal and natural as it once did. She will be wearing the collar for at least six or eight more weeks. She can start her chemotherapy as soon as she is released from the hospital."

"She will be in the hospital for at least seven to ten days. She will be in recover for an hour or so at which time they will have you come back and see her".

When they started sweeping the floor and turning off the lights we were once again worried that something was going wrong. The desk attendant finally told us that he would go back and see when we could go back. He returned and told us she will be in room 913 in just a few minutes we can go up there and see her.

We arrived at the room shortly after she did. Wow!!!! What a difference. She had no tubes coming out of her nose. She was awake and greeted us with a big smile. Totally not as I expected. She was no worse for wear.   I once again handed over the chattering, traveling teeth.

CHAPTER SEVEN
Chemotherapy

The first chemotherapy treatment was scheduled January 24th. Mom had been accepted into a clinical trial. Every Tuesday she was to be at the cancer center bright and early where she received her blood work and then a series of pills. These pills were spaced out over a four hour period.

We started to see a pattern after the treatments. We would return home and by dinner time that evening she became nauseous and threw up. We told ourselves out with the bad in with the good. We were also of the assumption that everything would have to get worse before it could get better. So far, tolerable at best.

First follow up visit with Dr. France went well. He wanted her to have radiation due to the fear he had of the tumor doing further damage to the neck. He didn't want to have to ever go back in and try to repair these bones again. So he consulted with the

Oncologist who reluctantly agreed to a very small "whiff" of radiation.

The first series of chemo was completed in four weeks and then a week of only the Revlimed pill. These pills were mailed to the house with the specific instruction that they be handled only by individuals who were not of child bearing years. This was to accelerate the potency of the trial cancer drug that was given every Tuesday. The next symptom or indication that something was going wrong was some slight ankle swelling. I phoned the Oncologist, Dr Hamadani, who reluctantly prescribed a very low dose diuretic. One pill was given that same evening with very little results. The next morning not only were her feet swollen but she had developed a rash. As the day went on her rash and edema seemed to be much worse so another call was made and they wanted to see her right away. We drove to the cancer center and by the time we arrived her blood pressure was so low it was almost undetectable. She was direct admitted to Ruby Memorial. During the next five days there were fluids given to increase her blood pressure which also increased her swelling.

During this time of being bedfast with pressure on her rear we began to notice that her butt was becoming worse and worse. The tiny little shearing that they tried to blow off at Healthsouth became an issue. The solution was to turn her every two hours to get her off of it. She wasn't on a spit so it

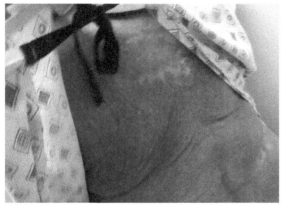 was not that easy given her increasing weight from the fluid. Her mobility became affected by the sudden weight gain. So she was laying most of the time on this ever growing, angrier and angrier pressure ulcer. We were flagging anyone down we could to please take a look at this from the dietician to the janitor but all they could come up with was the paper clock on the wall with left and right written at every two hour interval.

The labs during this hospitalization determined that her protein was nonexistent and that the fluid would not go away without adequate protein levels. Her chemo most likely destroyed the protein in her body. Unfortunately her diet was not helping. She was not a meat eater. Having no appetite didn't help either.

Several physicians and social workers met with us in the room to discuss her nutrition or lack of nutrition. We instantly took the offensive "we aren't trying to starve our mother, please don't take her away from us" We instantly felt like we had dropped the ball. We had no idea she wasn't getting her proper nutrition. So much nausea, vomiting and diarrhea over the past few weeks had left her with fear of eating. We thought the kind thing to do was not force her and she would eventually eat when she got hungry.

When she was discharged to home on February 13th the physician's assistant very adamantly told us that her swelling was not ever, ever going to go away and Mom would never go back to the weight she was. Her protein levels were just way to low.

From that day forward we set out to prove her wrong. We began our quest for protein. We needed to find enough grams of daily protein that she would not only be willing to consume but in a small enough volume to not make her feel over fed. This was not a small task. It was necessary to try to not only have her recommended daily allowance but to have enough to build back the deficit.

Putting her clothes on was quite a feat. She was beginning to lose control of her bowel functions due to the horrific tailbone ulcer and constant uncontrolled diarrhea. With an adult diaper and a pair of skin tight sweat pants that were stretched to the max she resembled a large blowup doll and was just as flexible. Her knees would not bend to get into the car so with the seat back as far as it would go and a thick gel cushion we were once again headed back home.

CHAPTER EIGHT
The Staffing

We were fortunate enough to have our sister-in-law Darlene step-up and be available for daytime care at home. Without her Mary and I would not be able to keep our jobs. This was yet another obstacle we needed to overcome. "What do we do about going to work? We cannot leave her alone she is virtually helpless. We have Aunt Dot at home who needs a lot of care as well. At 92 she does great but how long can she be trusted to not burn the house down?" We must hire a staff.

We were doing well with Darlene during working hours so we could hold down our jobs but what about our own home life? When do we get to do laundry and make dinner and go shopping and clean our house? We then hired Margaret.

Radiation started on February 20th. This was to be done every day for 10 days. On the 9th day of radiation, while on the table the incision in the back of mom's head began to leak fluid.

Sonny and Darlene were the ones who took her for the appointment this particular day. I had to work so Sonny asked Darlene to go along. With the ever worsening tailbone ulcer and the lack of bowel control he was not prepared to handle any toileting issues. "That was a woman's job"

When Sonny called me at work to report that they were sending her directly from the radiation oncology office to Dr. France's Office I was certain that they were overreacting. "Her bandage was wet from her shower that's all" "But….since you are taking her over please have someone look at her butt."

Unfortunately it was the worst possible scenario yet again. Her incision from her neck surgery had gone bad. Her inability to lie any way but flat on her back had caused a pressure ulcer to the back of her head where the doctor had attached to hardware to her skull. Oh yes, and the butt was in need of debridement. "Why didn't we have someone look at this earlier? " Dahhhhh!! " We will need to call in plastics". She is once again going to be a direct admission. "I'll pick up Mary and be right up".

Dr. France scheduled emergency surgery for the next day. I had hoped that they would do the tailbone also since she would be asleep but they needed the plastic surgery team to do it. They were only able to take a peek and give their opinion.

Dr. Casuccio was in charge of her wound care case along with his assistant Janice Shreve. They were wonderful with treating the wounds but not optimistic of her healing.

Dr. France debrided her head wound and cleaned up the damaged tissue. Mom returned from surgery with a wound vac attached to the back of her head. This was a very heavy and noisy piece of equipment designed to help promote healing. But this is a very heavy and noisy piece of equipment to be connected to.

The water weight continued to increase. This had an adverse effect on her hearing as well. As the edema grew worse her hearing became worse. We literally had to yell for her to hear us.

The heaviness of her ever plumping legs caused her walking to be difficult. Her inability to get up and walk around caused the edema to grow worse.

We were still on the good one day bad the next schedule. Still hoping we were at the worst of it. If it were to get worse before it gets better please let this be the worse.

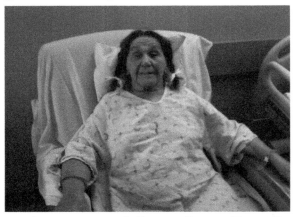 Plastics decided to do the butt debridement at the bedside twice, once on Monday, and once on Thursday. Dr. Casuccio said "well, we got her out of trouble".

Next day Dr. France decided to drill a few bore holes in mom's skull to try to promote some tissue growth. So…after this surgery Mom returned to us sporting a second vacuum line this one attached to her bottom. How cumbersome can it get?

Dr. Casuccio, during a morning round while I was at work and Sonny on duty at the hospital, asked point blank "where are you guys going with this? Just how far do you want to take this treatment? The chances of her healing are slim to none. Radiated tissue does not heal.

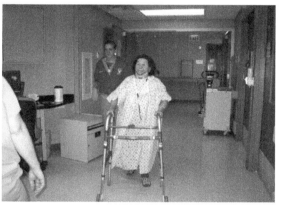

We were bound and determined to prove them wrong. We brought daily protein and tried our best to encourage her to eat. We brought Broccoli Cheddar soup from McDonalds as well as Bob Evans, Kentucky Fried Chicken, Wendy's Chili, Sheetz Hot Dogs, homemade bean soup you name it we tried it. No appetite!!! We encouraged daily walks out in the hall for at least no less than four laps around the hospital floor.

Discharged to home after 19 days on March 19th and once again I was faced with stretching her clothing over her ever growing body.

The wound vac team arrived at the house to do an assessment and instruct the nurse on the proper placement of the two wound vac hoses. This will need to be changed every three days. It took over an hour to complete the first vacuum attachment. I was becoming more annoyed by the minute. "Please let her sit up for the rest of the dressing change she can't lay on her side that long with her neck hurting" Still even being tortured in this manner she remained smiling and pleasant. I don't know how she does it.

No complaints from mom so how can we ever turn our back on her. We are in this nightmare no matter the outcome. Somehow we have to try to maintain our own life. We are in a "virtual ground hog day".

CHAPTER NINE
One Obstacle after Another

As if she hadn't been through enough, just four days after being discharged from the hospital she began getting more and more fluid filled and on March 23rd she bounced back into the hospital for yet another eight days. This was somewhat uneventful according to my recollection and on March 30th she was discharged to home still sporting two wound vac hoses and a whopping 160 pounds. One third of this being fluid.

Unfortunately, after we left the house on March 23rd for the hospital, Darlene was dressing mom's bed with fresh linen and her knee popped. We lost our primary care giver. Back to the drawing board we placed an ad and held a few interviews. This is when we hired Jenny.

Jenny was a retired cook. We thought that since appetite was one of our biggest obstacles, food should be our new focus.   I was handy to the house with my office being just three short minutes away so I could still monitor the blood sugar, draw up the insulin and be on call for emergencies.

During this period of time we were dealing with incontinence, hearing loss, two wound vac attachments, daily IV antibiotics…..we were borderline, running a skilled nursing home out of the house. I don't know how we did it. Looking back this was a very industrious undertaking.

CHAPTER 10
Have We Hit Rock Bottom Yet?

Follow-up with Dr. France was scheduled for April 5th. Still with little or no healing and being unable to hear a thing I'm still wondering if we have turned the corner and headed in the right direction. Can it really get much worse? Here she is swollen like a toad, deaf as a stone with large gaping holes in her head and tailbone, she had absolutely no appetite. Are we at rock bottom yet? Can we start to get better now?   NO!! Not yet!!!

On April 9th I left the house after my daily noontime dressing change and spoke with the visiting nurse who was there to change the wound vac, all vitals were within normal limits. I arrived back at my desk and within 10 minutes received a call to come back immediately.   I heard the ambulance and actually arrived just behind it as it pulled into the wrong driveway. I jumped from the car and asked who they were looking for and of course as I suspected it was for mom.

I got into the house and found my mom completely blue. Apparently the fluid had shifted when she lay back in bed and had applied too much pressure to her lungs and heart. I watched in horror as the medics worked and shouted "stay with us Delores!! Please hang on!!" Helpless, I could do nothing but pray and walk away and cry. During this mad dash from ambulance to bedside and back by medics and EMT's dear Auntie Dot continued to channel surf and ramp up the television volume to 100%. It's really for the best that she was spared this horrific scene.

The ambulance was obligated by the seriousness of the situation to proceed to the closest hospital which was Uniontown. Ruby was not an option. They did not have the additional 30 minutes to travel. I followed the ambulance out of the driveway but deliberately held back. I didn't want to be there when they took her dead body out of the ambulance. I honestly felt this was the end of the line. I was scared to death.

After picking up Mary and arriving at the hospital parking lot. We hurried into the ER and much to our surprise found mom sitting up and smiling. "Where have you girls been?"

The doctor told us they were running a few tests and she seemed to be stable and able to be transferred to Ruby. So once again we followed the ambulance to Ruby.

Ten more days in the hospital with her weight still up her hearing still gone her wounds still not healing and hope dwindling we were approached by social services and the team of young doctors who were more likely than not given the unpopular task of telling us that they had nothing more to offer. I guess they also need experience with dealing with distraught families. Maybe they just drew the short straw. We were summoned to the conference room where we were asked what we thought we would be expecting with moms future. They would like to talk to her and ask her wishes. Does she want to be a full code or a DNR (Do Not Resuscitate)? Does she have a living will or a medical power of attorney? Can they talk to her, does she understand? "Sure, you can talk to her but she can't really hear a thing?"

"Try to find a hearing device and we will meet you at 1:00 PM tomorrow and we will all talk to her together"

Next day came and it felt like going to the gallows. We had found a cheap hearing amplifier at the drug store after searching and making calls. We were waiting in the room with Sonny and Ray when the room filled with young "yes, I drew the short straw" doctors. They very quietly and somewhat gently asked mom her wishes. They proceeded to tell her the bad news that they would be offering no more chemo, no more radiation, no more surgery. She would be not getting better. They told her that she had experienced cancer of the neck and that the radiated skin would not heal. They told her that the extreme swelling would not be going away.

She looked them right in the eye when they asked her if she understood. She nodded understanding and said "I know but, thank God I'm in good health".

CHAPTER ELEVEN
Prayer, Positive Thinking and Protein

The doctors asked what would make her life more pleasant and of course she wanted the cumbersome wound vac removed from her head and butt. This would make movement easier and hopefully she can get out of bed and get a little more exercise.

They changed mom's status to DNR, had her sign a living will stating she would expect no heroic measures to extend her life. It seemed so final, yet surreal at the same time.

The next morning they sent in a Hospice Nurse to speak with Mom. This was something we felt was extremely inappropriate. I was actually in the car driving up to the hospital when the nurse called my cell phone and said she wanted to meet with me. Imagine my surprise to find out she was calling to arrange hospice care.

Sorry, your services are not required.

You would think with the doctors all being so negative we would be completely deflated....but I believe this gave us even more impetus to prove them wrong.

This woman was cooking Thanksgiving dinner a few short months ago, driving a car, volunteering at church, we were not about to give up without a fight. Ramp up the protein!

Call it denial or call it great faith but we were not giving up that's not how we roll. Yeah, we got handed lemons now we are going to make lemonade.

We were instructed to keep the gaping wounds as clean as possible. Shower everyday making sure we direct lots and lots of water into the wounds. They all seemed to chuckle when stupid me, in an effort to lighten the moment, asked "Where does all this water go? I don't want to spray it on the back of her head and have it come out her mouth". They assured me it wouldn't come out of her mouth. I still to this day wonder just where it does go.

I took graphic photos of the wounds. The head wound was particularly unsightly with not only the scull bone showing but the metal plate completely visible. The butt wound was large enough to put your fist in. The bone also completely exposed. No wander they were all so negative. Mom was in dire straits.

We were instructed to pack the butt wound with morphine gel and gauze for comfort. The chances of this type of wound ever progressing, was slim to none. It is considered Osteomyelitis and quite deadly. Once the bone is exposed there is really nothing that can be done. Her nutrition will play a factor. Since she has no appetite and does not even like protein foods we have actually reached an insurmountable obstacle.

With her neck fixed in one direction and unable to tilt her head all pills were crushed and given in applesauce. This has been what we have needed to do since the first day in Preby.

We were using adult diapers because the morphine and the tailbone wound masked the sensation needed to control her bowels. The antibiotics and the medications caused continual diarrhea. So we were seldom ever able to actually hit the commode without a clean-up. We were doing a load of towels and a load of underwear every day.

It's important for us to remember these trials because these are things we have now overcome. Praise the Lord!!!

CHAPTER TWELVE

Growing grass on a rock

Hearing was still an issue at this point and before the last hospital discharge the ENT team rolled the equipment into mom's room and did the office procedure that they had wanted to do each and every time she was sent home. The opportunity never arrived because prior to each appointment she bounced back into the hospital. They discovered that the fluid behind the ear drums was causing the hearing loss. We were scheduled for a follow up visit and they would be placing tubes in her ears to drain the fluid.

The tubes were placed on April 26th and what do you know…..she can hear!

We visited every four weeks with the plastic surgery team and the orthopedics. Upon one visit Mom was so confused that she asked me every five minutes where we were going and who we were going to see and asked why. I told her Dr. France. Every five minutes she would say who am I seeing? I said "Just remember it's a country" "Oh yeah" she replied "Dr. Spain". Was she just messing with me?

After seeing the plastic surgeon, Dr.Cassucio, the same day he merely shook his head and said "I see no change". Janice Shreve who has been our right hand gal from the day we met her asked if we could switch up the dressings to a different product and see what happens. So we began to use a one piece plastic dressing with a Sulfamylon cream for the head wound and a Poly Prisma disc inserted into the tailbone wound.

This regimen was religiously followed for the next four weeks and voila. We finally began to see what the surgeons were looking for "tissue granulation". Small at first but we couldn't wait for Janice to see.

When Janice came into the room and began to uncover the head wound we were holding our breath and waiting to see her reaction. We were not disappointed. She said "I'm going to get the boss."

By the look on Dr. Cassucio's face we knew our beliefs were true.

Suddenly, there will be lab work to be done and plans to be made. We left that day with a brand new hope. Mom is going to lick this thing.

Mom was set up for a reevaluation with her Oncologist, Dr. Hamadani. She was sent for x-rays and lab work.

It was no surprise to us to find out that there were no other issues with the bones and that the cancer was in remission.

No doubt about it with no appetite the secret to the healing was the protein shakes. This process was equivalent to a chemistry experiment. We found a protein powder that had the highest concentration of protein grams. Now with the water weight finally gone the actual weight was extremely low…..so we needed calories. The blood sugar was bouncing all over the place so we needed to reduce the sugar. Her belly won't hold much so this high calorie, low sugar, high protein concoction needed to fit in a coffee cup. My mad scientist sister went to the drawing board and with pen in hand figured out that with a yogurt as a base added to the protein powder and the sugar free nutrition powder combined with her favorite flavors of chocolate, strawberry and peanut butter she devised a shake that was not only low in volume but totally complete with nutrients and absolutely delicious.

This shake production became another of our daily duties. We now need a day off!!!!!!!

CHAPTER THIRTEEN
The Challenge

With progress finally being made we were finally able to return to our daily jobs. We can now let our guard down to some degree…..but now what? She can hardly be left alone. We are not wealthy how do we provide round the clock care and still have our own life? I hear about similar dilemmas every day at work. When you are faced with a sudden family crisis you have to come up with a doable plan.

With a few social events coming up for us we needed a trusted employee that could help out over the weekend. The constant nonstop planning and care of mom had taken its toll on home and family life. This needed fixed.

We are now faced with damage control. We cannot neglect our work…..but we have. We cannot neglect our families……but we have.　We cannot neglect our friends…….but we have.　Life as we know it has not been the same.　I remember being told that eight months ago by a physician that I didn't really want to believe. Sometimes it's difficult to process facts that we don't want to accept.

We placed another ad and found Helen. Helen is a retired nurse who has a love for older people and a few spare hours she needed to fill.　She was willing to take the day shift over the weekend and stay over if we had over night plans.　This freed us up to take a long weekend mini vacation to Skyline Drive in Virginia.　We were able to attend a wedding and a few summer picnics.

If we could rewind time and then fast forward to today we would see clearly just how much progress we have made.

It's only been eight short months, but on the other hand it's been eight long months. Mom is still having a good day and then a bad day.

On Sunday July 15th Mom and I returned to church.　You would have thought that a true to life celebrity had dropped in. After her many friends and neighbors lined up and gave her and I a hug the service leader opened with the announcement that "Our Delores is in the house". After cheers and applause the opening hymn was *Amazing Grace* and you guessed it I stood there with tears streamed down my face. Mom looked up at me and said "What's the matter with you?" "I've got something in my eye mom, something in my eye".

CHAPTER FOURTEEN
Miracle of miracles

If a lesson is to be learned by reading this story, it should be to never give up. Daily, families are faced with hard decisions and seemingly insurmountable odds. In many cases you have no choice but to play the cards you are dealt. But......I'm here to tell you that miracles happen every day. Where there is life there is hope.

My first actual undeniable miracle happened nearly fifteen years ago. My mom's older sister had been diagnosed with a deadly form of lung cancer. After her hospitalization her family doctor who incidentally was my boss at the time established that the x-rays and biopsies had confirmed the diagnosis and she would be requiring radiation. She said "Hey, doc I want another x-ray. I prayed about it and I think you should order another x-ray." He told her that he didn't want to delay her treatment any further but.....if you insist. I still get goose bumps when I remember taking the report off of the fax machine. It read… and I quote….." the lung nodule when compared to previous report shows total resolution".

Everyone I've told this story to has been simply blown away. I have copies of the x-ray reports.   It was nearly fifteen years ago and she is still with us. Still leading by example. Still full of faith and still giving credit where credit is due.

Ten years ago she overcame a sinus condition that was diagnosed as lymphoma. After being hospitalized for a week and being told there was nothing else to offer…..we found a doctor willing to try a very dangerous operation to debride those decaying sinuses. After completing six weeks of intravenous chemotherapy and about six months of good care at home with my mother, she was once again driving a car.

She experienced good health and a wonderful quality of life until a car accident put her down again. A young woman ran a stop sign and hit her broadside as she was driving a van load of family member's home from a church meeting. First words out of her mouth when we arrived at the hospital…."It was not my fault" She wanted each and everyone to know that this accident was not her error. It's usually automatically assumed that the 90 year old driver is most likely at fault. Not in this case the young woman admitted running the stop signs.

She ordered the EMT's and Medics around that evening and they never realized the extent of her injuries because she was that good at hiding her own pain. Once again always concerned about others over her own self.

Her hip was broken and required a total replacement. The naysayers all said "Poor Dorothy she will never walk again." I honestly looked at them and said "You don't know her very well do you"?

After a few weeks rehab and several months living with my mom she was once again back home and driving her own car.

Miracle number four for Dear Auntie occurred on Father's Day 2010. We were enjoying a picnic lunch at my son Michael's house when I got the most uneasy feeling. I just couldn't shake it. I told mom, "Have you talked to Aunt Dorothy today?". She said "No, she is in church I usually don't talk to her until evening." "We really should call her" so on the way home from Michael's we tried several times to reach her she did not answer her house phone or her cell phone. We became more and more concerned so we called her stepson who lives next door he thought she was at mom's house so he did not get at all concerned about not seeing her out and about all day. He immediately ran over left himself in with his key and found her laying on the floor. She had 46 unsuccessful cell phone call attempts that she had made as well as a few random pictures of the floor. She was extremely incoherent and was reciting the Lord's Prayer nonstop. This episode remains a mystery to us because the diagnosis was something I had never heard of before they are calling it "broken heart syndrome". At a cardiology follow up appointment the doctor said she was his eighth case since opening his practice earlier that year.

She was recovering very nicely at mom's when mom became sick. She remains with us today and is a joy and blessing to our family.

The moral of the story

I sincerely believe I was destined to write this story as an inspiration to everyone who has been dealt a tough hand of cards.

Sadly, if you haven't had to deal with the illness of a close family member someday you will.

There is light at the end of the tunnel. We shall overcome. Nothing is impossible with God. If you have faith the size of a mustard seed. I'm running out of clichés.

You need to always look to the brighter side of every situation. I try to really never get down. I truly believe that in the near future my mom will be back on her feet and taking care of us all again.

I dropped my car of at the garage for a repair yesterday and she was not available to come and pick me up. Wow....I've taken her for granted. She was always there for us. Always willing to help us out. The word "no" was not in her vocabulary.

Cherish the times you have with your loved ones. When you leave them for the day or tuck them in bed at night ask yourself what it would feel like if "life as you know it would never be the same". If you were saying goodbye or good night for the last time make it count. No regrets. No harsh words. No fights.

Healing can happen. With proper care, which includes lots and lots of positive thinking, add prayers from every church in the tri-state area regardless of denomination and several gallons of protein, and you can achieve miracles.

Unfortunately we don't possess a crystal ball. We don't really know what we have in our future. We can't predict if this illness is going to take her from us. We only know that we have this day and this day only. We must make the best of each day that we can enjoy each other's company.

This is not only true of our aging and ill family members but of the ones we least suspect. Your loved one can be snatched from you at any time or any place.

Don't ever allow yourself to feel the guilt of remembering that the last conversation you had with a loved one was a quarrel. Many times I've heard the saying "Treat each day as if it were your last".

I dedicate this story to the strong powerful women that have influenced my life and made me who I am today.

I have been blessed with a wonderful mother, a fantastic aunt and an amazing mother-in-law.

Sadly, we didn't have any tough decisions to make regarding my mother-in-laws care. When she was stricken with side effects of radiation treatments for her advanced cancer she never came home from the hospital. She would have wanted it that way. She never wanted to be dependent on anyone.

In a tremendous show of solidarity her nine grandchildren linked arms and marched together into the Intensive Care Unit to say there final goodbyes to their beloved grandmother. The ICU nurses told us that the end will not be anything like what you see on TV. There will be no drama or production.

When the monitors became silent and the screen went to flat line the entire family surrounded the bed and suddenly as if on cue we all began to sing one of her favorite old hymns "May the Circle be Unbroken". Not a dry eye in the house that includes nurses, doctors, orderlies and aids. They scattered to every available nook and linen closet.

I miss her to this day. She gave me a gift on her death bed that I will never forget. She somehow mustered up enough energy to say "Hey" as I was turning to walk away. When I turned to her she flashed the biggest broadest smile I had ever seen. It was a smile of approval and appreciation meant for me and me alone. I will cherish that moment. It was unspoken but it said volumes. Her beautiful smile is imbedded in my mind and I see it every time I think of her.

Always remember that mountains can be moved against overwhelming odds if you apply the principles of Prayer, Positive Thinking and Protein.